A REAL KILLING

Also by William Keegan

Consulting Father Wintergreen

A
Real
Killing

a novel by
William Keegan

St. Martin's Press
New York

to Veronica Parker and Henry Woolf

I

If you want to make money in this world you've got to go to where the money is. I got the message one Sunday morning some years ago. At the time I had been staggering under the weight of those Sunday papers, and paused for breath – I had a flat in London at the top of a Georgian terrace house which consisted mainly of stairs.

The middle of the *Sunday Times* fell out – the thing they call the Business News – and before you could say 'Derek Terby', there he was: Derek Terby, the greyest man I have ever met in my life, four square on the front page in glorious monochrome.

I'd better explain. You're probably familiar with the theme milked to death by most of the great writers – Shakespeare, Proust, Tolstoy and lesser mortals like Anthony Powell and Leslie Charteris. You know: People Keep Turning Up In Your Life. You can't get away from them for longer than ten years at most, and even if you do they haunt you at night in those perpetual roll calls of past failures we call our dreams. Last night, for instance, I was woken up in the middle of the roll call of the first year at my grammar school. There it was, loud and clear, Proctor, Quisling, Roberts, Terby. Terby.

Terby. What a name for a central character. Sounds like a pained groan from the dentist's chair, or one of those early Graham Greene villains. Anyway, there was Terby, Derek's familiar smirk, leaping out of the *Sunday Times* Business News, with the usual gruesome caption favoured by those financial journalists – I know them: I'm one of the breed myself – 'The Terby Touch Swings It Again'.

There followed a nauseating piece about how Terby had just made another million or so by buying some defunct company, and 'selling off' [sic: you never use one word in the financial world where two will suffice] its 'Plum property sites at a fantastic premium above book value'. And so on. You know the sort of rubbish. I turned over to the gossip column and my worst fears were confirmed. There it was: a fulsome sycophantic five hundred words about the great god Terby, spewed out of the gushing mouth of some young pup who would no doubt be applying for a job in the Terby outfit on the Monday.

Well, I ask you. How would *you* feel if you'd been at school with a fairy like Terby and you found that the young jerk had made a million while you were still trying to pay off your university debts? Sorry: 'fairy' is a misnomer, Terby was not distinguished for his abilities in any direction, as far as we and the local convent knew. In fact he was so inconsequential, so bloody thick, that it is a wonder he managed to scrape through 'O' levels before finally being thrown out. Which he was. The fact that his name is now prominent on the Appeal writing paper is just another proof of a certain religious order's ability to cut its cloth to suit the bank balance.

I'd better insert a few points about myself. If you want to understand *anything* about anybody else – a matter on whose feasibility we solipsists have grave doubts – you have to know a little about the standpoint of the man who is telling you. Objectivity is so subjective these days that you can never be sure you're getting the truth from anybody – whether it's from the horse's mouth, the newspaper which feeds on it, the periodical that purports to give you a 'depth analysis' or the subsequent historian who interprets the lot. Personally, I believe things when I believe them, and not before.

Anyway the story I'm now going to relate is true, and the only reason why I'm relating it is that deep-seated desire within us all to boast or confess – call it what you will – our misdeeds to someone. Only in this case expediency dictates that I should not go running to the police with my tale, and my attempt to purge my soul by making a clean breast of it to the Jesuits simply backfired. My confessor, a Father Wintergreen, interjected with increasing frequency, and eventually pulled back the black confessional curtain saying: 'Come come, Tarquin, this really won't do. I'm paid to forgive real sins, not the imaginary exploits of some vicarious saint.'

I thought of dressing this account up in fictional form – to make it more plausible – but decided against it. I've got nothing against literature myself, except that nobody ever reads it. The way to get fiction sold these days you've got to do it the Harold Robbins or Arthur Hailey way – a huge superstructure of half-baked conventional characters, and plenty of detail – preferably of the sort you've never experienced yourself. You've also got to do it in about 598 pages, which is far too long and complicated. So there's none of that sort of crap in this account, although I've had to change the names of people and institutions to protect the guilty.

2

Now, I promised to say a few words about myself. I'm six feet two – I hope heights are never metricated – and weigh thirteen stone. You can get a general idea of what I looked like at the time from the fact that when I turned up at the *Morning Jet* Financial Page for my first job, the office boys started cracking jokes about the Messiah. Jesus didn't wear spectacles, but that's not the sort of pedantic anachronistic detail to worry the office boys on the *Morning Jet*.

I got into journalism by a process of elimination. I'd always suffered from verbal diarrhoea, and for a long time fancied myself as a barrister. Attendance at one session at the Old Bailey cured me of the influence of a thousand courtroom films however – how do those guys manage to keep awake in there? – so I decided it had to be the written word for me. I was reading economics at Cambridge at the time, and thought financial journalism would be a neat way of combining my ambitions with my qualifications. It would have been, if I had obtained my qualifications; but I ploughed my degree. The trouble with working-class lads who fight their way up to university is that they tend to relax when they get there; but that's another story. Luckily the Financial Page of the *Morning Jet* was very relaxing in itself – it had to be with about three inches of space but an empire-building financial editor who had managed to acquire a staff of twelve writers. I therefore had plenty of time for study, and took my First during office hours at London University. But that was just to salve my pride; my feelings about economics had always been ambivalent – how do you like a discipline which has made only one real discovery in a hundred years, namely the time Keynes realised that to solve the unemployment problem you have to send people back to work? I ask you.

So there I was, single and in my late twenties, earning several thousand a year, and living in this top-floor pad in Canonbury Square, Islington.

The work was chicken feed: writing about how Shell had increased its dividend or ICI was going to expand, mostly from handouts, with the occasional scoop thrown in, usually as a result of information gathered at one of the hundreds of free lunches I attended in plushy West End hotels as part of my work.

My colleagues were a mixed collection of graduates and ex-office boys, most of whom regarded the place as a stepping stone to the stockbroker's office where they would make their real fortune. I myself had no idea where my stepping stones were leading, but after almost thirty years of total poverty I was quite content for a while to have a job which paid off my university debts and provided me with enough credit cards to take out the procession of girls one goes through at that age.

I therefore found my real objections to the job lying dormant for a while. For consider the position of a poor scholarship lad, brought up to hate the Tories and all they stand for, a passionate believer in social justice. What was I doing writing for a page whose raison d'être was tipping shares and advising the better off on how they could be even better off?

What contribution was I making to solve the housing problem, feeding the hungry and generally practising all those beatitudes Father Wintergreen had stuffed down my throat at school? You've got it: in the phrase so beloved of that master of understatement, the British academic: bugger all.

My conscience was really pricked by Mrs Cordoba. It certainly emerged unscathed from periodic encounters with my father, who after indoctrinating me with all those socialist ideals in his youth, finally threw in the towel on retirement, and throughout my stay on the Financial Page kept pressing me for share tips.

Mrs Cordoba, however. Boy, was she different. It all happened in the usual chicken-hearted way we rediscover our true feelings. After reading that nauseating pap about Derek Terby in the *Sunday Times* Business News I had been – irony of ironies – detailed by my boss, Augustus Tring, to do a follow-up piece for Monday's *Jet*. Fortunately although you suffered under Tring's tutelage from the fact that everything written by the staff appeared under *his* name, at least you were spared the indignity of attaching your own by-line to the sort of rubbish I had to write about Terby that day.

That Sunday evening – I remember it was May, because my girl friend likened the blossom to confetti and I got worried – I threw out a few passing swear words on the subject of Terby to this girl. Her name was Lindy Fanshawe, if I recall correctly, and she wasn't really interested in marriage : she had too many other boy friends for that, as I later discovered.

'Terby?' she said. '*Derek* Terby?'

'Yes, that's him. IQ of ninety. Bank balance of one million.'

'I met him last night. At a party given by my landlady. He's a friend of the Cordobas.'

We were sitting in the basement flat in St Johns Wood, which Lindy shared with another girl – an air hostess who was always conveniently in Bombay or some such place. It would be misleading to say the Cordobas lived upstairs, because George Cordoba had moved out ages ago into the Dorchester – whether in pursuit of his sexual diversions, or in flight from his wife's I have never discovered. I told you this would be an honest account. Mrs Cordoba had already been built up into the sort of mystery force I had made a mental note to climb upstairs and conquer some time. Lindy – no mean performer herself – regarded her as the ultimate in femmes fatales, and was always asking me if I'd met her landlady, without ever actually introducing us. Tonight I had dropped in unexpectedly, and in retrospect I realised that Lindy was trying to get rid of me fast.

'Come upstairs and I'll introduce you to her,' says Lindy to your unwary narrator.

We had to go up the basement steps and knock at the front

door. St Johns Wood is crawling with those huge stuccoed and porticoed houses which just fall short of embassy status but which are good enough for the likes of most of us. I don't mind telling you, I rather enjoyed the St Johns Wood phase of my life. Love affairs are all very well, but there's something to be said for conducting them in the right places, and from then on Earls Court was out.

Mrs Cordoba showed us in, pushed me towards the booze cupboard, and walked over to the window.

'Pour out some of that Bacardi. I'll have a very large one.'

I fumbled my way through the honours, with a vague feeling of excitement which was heightened by Lindy's sudden announcement that she must go. Mrs Cordoba had opened the window and gone out onto the balcony. 'One of the sad things about this house is that one is surrounded by members of the rag trade, who treat their poor little au pairs like scullions.' She came back into the room, and lowered herself with great precision onto the carpet. I can't remember much about my initial impression of the room, because I was much too interested in my initial impression of her. I recall being caught turning up the edge of the carpet, and her saying: 'My dear boy, that's a cheap way of telling an expensive Persian rug. You should never let yourself be seen doing that.' Then she looked – dreamily, I fancied – up into my eyes, and said: 'Sit down and tell me about yourself.'

I started gently, with a few half-truths, the drink talking freely on my empty stomach. After a few more drinks I found myself telling her tentatively about my political views – a sure way to a Girton girl's heart, but I wasn't at all sure about femmes fatales alive and living off Abbey Road.

3

I need not have worried about Mrs Cordoba's political views being an impediment to the fulfilment of our burgeoning relationship.

'But my dear boy you should not be so apologetic about your beliefs.'

She stroked her shimmeringly expensive dress – no, that's a misnomer : the only tremulous object in the room was myself, but you see what I'm trying to convey – looked up at the Picasso (genuine or good attempt) on the wall and continued : 'The only respectable thing to be these days is extremely left wing. I find your views well to the right of mine. Why you're almost a Gaitskellite.'

I must have looked nonplussed, as they say. Having attempted, as usual, to tread warily in this new farmyard, I was now laid bare as the chicken, Tandoori colour, that I really was. I attempted to redress the balance, move the ball out to the wing, as it were, and pretend that I had not made my real views clear earlier on.

She removed her cigarette holder at one mile an hour, shifted uncomfortably (for me) her physical position, and smiled a smile which – I offered myself mental odds of a hundred to one in favour – connoted an imminent leap into bed by the assembled cast.

'Forgive me. I must go and collect my step-children from Benediction. Why don't you buy me lunch on Wednesday. I shall be in the main entrance to Morley College at one o'clock sharp.'

That gave me something to look forward to, as my mother would have said. The following morning my daydreams on the subject of Mrs Cordoba were interrupted by Augustus Tring, during his 11 a.m. conference at the *Morning Jet* financial office. Conference time was when we had to produce our bright ideas, so that Tring could go off to lunch at the Savoy confident in the knowledge that, in the absence of news later in the day, he still had something to fill his column with. This morning, however, was more of a post mortem than an ideas session.

'Terence,' he said to me, 'how come that we were the only paper this morning which put Terby's proceeds from the sale of those property sites at £500,000 instead of £5 million. If he bought them at the book value of £1 million, according to your arithmetic he's actually made a loss. Where's this "fantastic premium" you write about?'

Yes, that was a Freudian slip all right. It was all very well being consumed with envy at Terby's success, but clearly these were not the sort of tactics which were going to get one anywhere. Now, it was conventional in the *Jet* office to blame anything – a bad telephone line, any colleague who was absent, even sunspots – rather than admit that you'd made a mistake. But I couldn't see my way out of this one, and conceded the point like a man.

For my penance I got the thing I most dreaded.

'The best way you can make amends Terence is to keep a close eye on Terby. I'm sure he's got something really big brewing. Chase him, talk to his chauffeur, sleep with his wife. Anything. But don't let anyone else scoop you.'

This of course was Tring having just seen a re-run of the Front Page and trying to behave like a newspaperman. What worried me was not all that rubbish, but the mere fact that I had now been assigned to following the man I most detested in this life – a role for which, in my calendar, there was strong competition, but which Terby won hands down.

In classical novels and smart biographies, people have regular confidantes. The likes of you and me, however, have to put up with the next person we talk to. During the following couple of day I was preoccupied with medical check-ups for a spot of back trouble, mistakenly attributed by one bluff houseman at Barts to 'too much of the other'. The next confidante who came up, as it were, was Mrs Cordoba, with whom I had a handsome lunch off the King's Road at the expense, naturally, of the *Morning Jet*. It was on this occasion that Mrs Cordoba acted as the catalyst who brought out my real feelings about the job.

'I think share-dealing is positively immoral,' she said. 'How can you possibly reconcile your political views with the pursuit of inside information for these awful readers of the *Morning Jet*. The thought is too abhorrent.'

'You're right. I must find something else.'

'You should be doing some form of social work.'

'Yes' (lamely).

'Of course, the best social and charitable work has traditionally been done by trusts set up by unscrupulous rogues who have made their pile first.'

'Yes. I hadn't thought of that.'

Given the state of the vibrations crossing that lunch table, Mrs Cordoba would have persuaded me of anything. I hadn't at that stage caught on to the fact that all this invisible make-up women wear these days conceals quite a lot. Here was a femme fatale, presumably in her thirties, comfortably redolent of Madame Rochas, and evidently aiming herself at me. Would it have occurred to you, in the same position, that her teenage step-children were in fact her real children, and that this tender lamb was forty-four if she was a day?

Perhaps it was because there was so much of a confessional and – I hoped – seductive atmosphere about the place that my mind was fully occupied, and I clean forgot Lindy Fanshawe's earlier remark that the Cordobas knew Terby. Anyway, as usual I blundered straight on.

'To crown it all,' I heard myself saying, 'the man whose financial career I now find myself reporting on is a frightful character I knew at school called Terby.'

'Derek Terby? But George [her husband] is on his Board.'

'Oh' (lamer still and lamer).

'They're up to something, you know, at this minute.'

'Oh. What?'

'I don't know. I don't see much of George these days. Let's take a taxi back to St Johns Wood.'

4

I honestly didn't know whether to make the event you're now expecting into the climax of the last chapter or the beginning of this. One has visions of those greasy little men who write railway station bestsellers going into great detail about imagined successes with their nine-to-five paper heroines, while in reality living a solitary life and suffering from Portnoy's other complaint. The prurient reader may be disappointed at this stage, because my first entrance to Mrs Cordoba's august groinal bower was so swift and shortlived that I had it all in a sentence, as you might say. She having no breasts to speak of, as I discovered beneath the architectural façade, we went straight to the matter in hand – I find it difficult not to be flippant about sex, being no Durrell, and I suppose you can say that again.

Not unexcited by the prospects ahead, I had managed nevertheless to stagger somehow from the taxi into the house, and then upstairs to George's side of the eight-foot-square bed. I had always thought that if they can manage to have bathrooms and bedrooms adjoining in Majorcan hotels, there's no reason why we English shouldn't afford ourselves the same treatment; and I'm delighted to report that the Abbey Road area did itself proud in that respect. Anyway, to get to that sentence, we disrobed, hopped onto the sixty-four square feet and did our stuff; leaving pre-coital caresses to the birds. Approximately four minutes later she sighed with apparent contentment and said: 'People always say I come like a factory girl.'

Naturally I made some stupid reply like 'Come again' or some such inanity, but I'll spare you the rest. People always say repartee is the reply you think of on the way home. My problem is that it's the reply I make at the time.

Anyway, having thus established our good intent, we were able to go downstairs to the Bacardi and Persian carpet room, and pour ourselves a celebratory drink.

'I shouldn't tell you this . . .' she began.

'Please don't.' I chanced my arm and narrowed my eyes, trying to keep the relationship on the facetious plane at which I usually feel more at home.

'Don't narrow your eyes like that, Terence,' she almost squirmed with distaste. 'They're narrow enough already, my darling.'

So they are. The product of some obscure Chinese ancestry down by the Liverpool docks. But let her continue: 'George and Derek Terby are planning something very big. I wouldn't understand the details – my adult education course only covers psychology, I believe – but there's going to be a large takeover.'

'Oh. I see.'

Now she was talking. My pulse rate was showing signs of real prurience. The big deal. The big scoop. Fame and recognition for Terence Aloysius Rachmaninov Quin (that's why they call me Tarquin: my initials, you see). Financial Journalist of the Year, without any shadow of a doubt.

'What's the other company called?'

'I don't know darling. I can't remember. Let's go upstairs again: I hear the factory sirens calling.'

5

With Mrs Cordoba providing a normal human dose of physical contact, I was not particularly put out when I learnt that I had been cuckolded – insofar as a bachelor can be – by a colleague in the office who had taken a big fancy to Lindy Fanshawe. Since I had now virtually moved in with her landlady, I could hardly complain at being evicted by the tenant. As it happened, the colleague was an old friend: new friends come and go, but old friends stay on for ever, even though one spends half one's time complaining about them to the new friends.

The news of my quasi-cuckoldom was actually a sort of comeuppance for my having boasted to Jack Spick about the Cordoba affair. As you will have guessed, it turned out that he knew the house quite well.

Spick and I had been at school together, in the same class as – full marks – Derek Terby. Spick it was who had first suggested my name to Augustus Tring as a potential recruit. A further word about Spick: we are all of us aware of the ironies and paradoxes of life, and they don't come much more paradoxical than Jack Spick. Brought up in the Guildford, Surrey, stockbroker belt, his father a highly successful tax lawyer, Spick had plenty of things to revolt against. But he believed in doing it in style. Not for him your actual dropping out into lice-ridden communes on Eel Pie Island, or the freakier scenes of North Islington. Oh no. Wherever he was the night before, whatever revolution he was preaching to oppressed victims of the capitalist system all over London, Spick liked to get a taxi back to Guildford and have breakfast in bed the following morning, dutifully served up by his loving Irish mum.

Working in the *Jet* City Office, and living almost entirely on *Jet* expenses (Yes: don't groan: we were known as the *Jet* set), Spick was able to finance his contribution to the revolution fairly comfortably. He didn't believe in buying shares – it was against the Trotskyist scheme of things – but he was one of the best share tipsters in the business, all conveniently under Tring's collective by-line of course, so that the comrades at meetings were given no occasion for offence. On his way to meet these comrades, he would naturally stop off at the Bacchus steak-house or somewhere, so as not to embarrass them publicly. But I'll say this for Jack Spick: he'd be the last to describe such conduct as hypocrisy.

We quickly buried the hatchet over the Lindy business, and that Friday lunchtime – after Jack had finished his 'Shares to Watch' column for the Monday paper – we had a couple of drinks in Birches. Birches was one of those City hostelries in an alley just off the Stock Exchange; it looked quaint to tourists with its sawdust at ground level and braying stockbrokers above, and we always found it a suitable place to grumble about the capitalist system in general and Augustus Tring in particular. Somehow those well-heeled thugs from the cast of 'If' were the perfect unwitting audience for our complaints, going on as they did about the need for a permanent wages policy while collecting forty grand or so themselves, one way and another. (Nowadays Birches consists entirely of sawdust: it's been demolished.)

On this occasion Spick was particularly irritated by some character who was all white collars, cuffs and his mother's face (we presumed) who after bellyaching for ten minutes about unions not doing an honest day's work for an honest day's pay, then proceeded to say he must leave and drive off to the country for a long weekend.

'That's bloody it. That's bloody typical of these upper-class jerks,' said Spick.

'I don't know Jack – probably lives in Guildford like yourself,' I ventured.

'Watch it, you traitor to the working class.'

I didn't rise to that one. I'd certainly been taken aback by Mrs Cordoba's casual remarks about my work. But then I'd also been influenced by her point that some of the greatest philanthropists had had a dubious past.

'If only we had enough cash to opt out of the whole bloody business,' said Spick.

'The same remark is being made all over the country this minute,' I said.

'While we've been drinking in this bar this morning, Derek Terby has probably made another £500,000 out of some shady deal or other.'

Terby. Terby. That set my easily led mind off again. Could I trust my old friend Spick with my scoop from Mrs Cordoba – or rather my half-scoop, because in spite of nosing around George Cordoba's study I had not yet managed to find out what this other company involved in the takeover was. Did it matter even if I couldn't trust him? Here we were, both lamenting our involvement in the bloody City . . .

'I remember when I first started this job,' Spick continued, 'I used to have a pub lunch with Terby – he was nothing in those days. I was short of stories for Tring, and Terby was always feeding me useful bits of information about companies. I couldn't understand why he was being so helpful. It was only later that I realised he was using me beautifully – getting the *Jet* to tip punk shares he'd bought for nothing, and selling out as soon as the *Jet* readers poured in.'

'I've heard that Terby is about to become involved in some big takeover,' said yours truly tentatively.

'Oh Christ, he's always involved in some big takeover. He daren't let that pyramid of pieces of paper he calls a financial empire stand still for two seconds, or it'll all collapse around his feet.'

Fair point, I thought. I didn't really have enough information even to think of sharing it with Spick at this stage. Meanwhile the conversation had conveniently drifted away from our guilt feelings, and there it stayed.

That afternoon my father telephoned me at the office to ask whether Rio Tinto Zinc – the mining firm, you may recall – was likely to cash in on the world's general shortage of resources, or go bust as a result of the ecology boom. I asked him whether he had any principles left, with all this share buying he was doing out of his old-age pension and accumulator winnings – the rich can gamble on the Stock Exchange, but the poor have to win on the horses before they start.

He cut me short: 'I don't know about principles, but I haven't got much money left. Every share you've given me since you persuaded me to play the stock market has gone down on bended knees. My basic system now is to do the opposite of what you recommend.'

Well, we can only do our best. Spick took Lindy off to Paris that weekend, as usual telling his old Irish mother that he was going with me. We were both of us pushing thirty, and anybody else in the world except Spick's mother would have been disturbed at the suggestion that her son always went on holiday with other boys.

But Mrs Spick had not yet given up hope that Jack might be ordained into the priesthood – although Father Wintergreen's reports to her had not been encouraging – and the only female she liked to associate with Jack's holidays was Holy Mother Church. At all events Spick and Lindy were well out of the way, and George Cordoba had flown to Nice with his secretary. With the Cordoba (step-)daughters safely away at school, that gave me the freedom of St Johns Wood and Mrs Cordoba for the weekend. This freedom was, of course, punctuated by the occasional visit to Brompton Oratory, because Mrs Cordoba, who fancied herself as something of a Mary Magdalene, believed that sex was the most forgivable of sins, and liked to give the clergy the chance to exercise their plenipotentiary powers of absolution.

6

Ever reflected that our very own Vaughan Williams liked adapting 'Greensleeves' so much that half of his other work sounds as though the orchestra is about to burst into the familiar sounds of 'Alas my love'? An exaggeration, no doubt, but perhaps I've got a point. Starling and I were sitting on the terrace in St Johns Wood listening to Radio Three's gentle approach to Sunday morning, and on our third or fourth cup of real coffee – a blend of Kenya, Brazilian and, almost, my finger: I wasn't too famliar with the kitchen machinery around those parts. Starling? Well, Mrs Cordoba is a well-known London bird, and was crying out for a pet name.

We'd been discussing John Stuart Mill's favourite dilemma – 'Shall we give liberty to the enemies of freedom', and I'd dropped in a few hackneyed quotes from other authors, such as Juvenal's 'Who's going to guard the guards?' She liked it. People who spend their entire lives socialising are impressed by anything which sounds as though it's come out of a book. The Morley College syllabus was having a hard time of it trying to keep up with her social routine. But she was regretting having put on a rather devastating dress, because I was losing interest in intelligent conversation already – we'd only been away from the sack for half an hour. Sensing this, she narrowed her lips in a not unthrilling way and said: 'Really Tarquin, there are other things in life. Don't you want me to tell you about that letter addressed to George that I opened last night?'

'Well, if you insist.'

'Wait a minute.'

My starling disappeared upstairs and returned a few minutes later carrying a letter and wearing loosely unflattering trousers.

'To assist your concentration my love,' she said. 'Now, I've made rather a hash of steaming open this letter, so you're going to have to copy the writing on the envelope, and drive down to Chelsea later on to an sw3 pillar box, where you can post it back here.'

'Ingenious,' I said. 'But can we match the writing paper?'

'Yes, my love. Fortunately I have a good selection of envelopes.'

'Spill the beans then,' I said, in pale imitation of phrases popular in my youth (not hers, you remember).

'It's from Lord Brachan, the merchant banker. Nobody ever puts anything interesting into letters these days, and all this says is Dear Cordoba, Thank you for your letter of the 10th. Of course I should be delighted to discuss any such proposal with you. Yours sincerely, Brachan.'

'Innocent enough,' I said.

'Innocent my foot. There's something going on. It's almost certainly to do with this takeover they're planning.'

I knew full well that the main reason she was telling me this, in accordance with the theory I mentioned earlier, was that I happened to be the nearest available confidante. So I said: 'Why are you telling me all this?'

'Partly because I have got to sell some shares and want to know what's really going on in Terby Holdings. Partly because it all relates to the general intrigue we're having. Do you love me?'

'No, but I love the situation' (I nearly said but deemed wise to keep to myself).

'Well, I er . . .'

'Relax Tarquin. Let's not talk about it. Now write out this envelope and we can post it on the way to Confession. I leave it to your professional genius to follow this up with Brachan.'

7

I should like to be able to boast at this stage that I had no illusions about Mrs Cordoba. You will no doubt have worked out
already that she was one of these women who, once their husbands
have virtually walked out on them – merely using the house as a
sort of left-luggage department – need an endless procession of
young men to convince them that they're still young and wanted.
They take even greater liberty with their age than most, and
think nothing of chopping fifteen years off the official birth certifi-
cate version where others would draw the line at five.

All of which is pathetic. But one's twenties are not necessarily
one's years of greatest sensitivity, and looking back on it perhaps
I should have handled the affair differently. On the other hand,
any regrets on this score can be accompanied by my mitigating
plea that the rides I was taken for by Mrs Cordoba assumed
several forms, and I had no idea of my real place in her large
and shifting hierarchy. But more of that later. Having had my
qualms of conscience about my job, I could shelve them for a bit,
and get on with the hunt for what Terby was up to, pursuing my
exotic affair with Mrs Cordoba en route.

One of the things which is meant to distinguish a stage farce
from a plausible and serious play is the number of chance oc-
currences and outrageous coincidences the author springs on the
audience. In real life we know that the distinction is unjust, and
quite long periods of boredom can be followed by the most amazing bursts of excitement when everything seems to go in our
favour and we have the most incredible chains of luck.

I kept quiet about my half-scoop at the Monday morning conference – there's no point in raising people's hopes unnecessarily, I reasoned – and had a few drinks with my stockbroking contacts, to see if they knew anything about Terby's latest interests. As usual they were full of stories about how he'd bought ten per cent of this company and twenty per cent of that, but there was nothing remotely resembling a takeover in the offing. One straw in the wind which I failed to grasp was a remark by John Crampton – an elegant fortyish stockbroker with pinched but handsome Michael Rennie style cheekbones. 'Render unto Terby the things that are Terby's,' he muttered, adding: 'Personally I should seek the Messiah in other parts.'

That afternoon Tring called me into his office. 'Terence: I've been lunching with Lord Brachan (pronounce Brawn). He's looking for someone to write a history of Blizzards. I told him I knew the ideal studious young man. His secretary is expecting you to ring.'

It might be useful if I were to remind you that I have had to change the names of the people involved in this story. Lord Brachan is the name I have given to a distinguished merchant banker at the time – a former Tory minister – who was very well known inside the City. I should add that merchant bankers have until recently been considered socially at least a cut above your ordinary Barclays or Lloyds – one of their great skills in those days was dispensing advice to companies on takeovers, and – not to put too fine a point on it – advising the companies concerned to give them a hefty commission in the process. The 'merchant' bit, with its connotations of financing the tea trade, has a nice exotic ring which these days means nothing.

I took it for granted that a guy like Brachan would be booked up for months ahead, and was rather surprised when his secretary gave me an appointment for 11 a.m. that Friday – a double bonus, because it would offer me a day's respite from having to think up absurd ideas for Tring's morning conference.

I was ushered into Brachan's parlour in one of the older City buildings by a flunkey who looked as though he was left over from the tea-trading days. His manner combined exaggerated respect for the institution which employed him with total contempt for its latest visitor.

Brachan was your usual tall languid aristocrat, Eton and the Guards and all that; unlike his minions, he immediately put me at my ease – looking pretty comfortable himself behind a perfect Georgian desk whose top was refreshingly barren of anything resembling a work-load.

Now in these post-war days in which the only common enemy is ourselves, you either like people or you don't, and we're all pretty hopeless at suppressing enmity or aggression. Anybody as up to his neck in high finance as Brachan, *must* be crooked to some extent, in my book, however disarming the posture he adopts for outsiders; and the Brachans of this world are actively encouraged by the rest of us to retain what we regard as their natural airs, whether they want to or not.

Yet I couldn't help liking this character, and I fancy from the fact that he didn't throw me out for two hours – an hour of his time must have been worth a few thousand – that he quite warmed to me.

Not that the official business of the meeting took much time. I'd prepared my negotiating position while shaving that morning, and decided that none of your establishment charm could compensate for hard cash, and that no history of Blizzards was going to be rattled out on *my* manual typewriter for less than a couple of grand.

Having outlined the great boring subject of the book, Brachan leaned back in his (Louis something) chair and said: 'Of course I suppose we'd have to pay you something for this. I forget [liar] whether I mentioned a fee to Tring. What would you want?'

'Well' (research, take it seriously, painstaking and diligent work, etc), 'I should have thought that, perhaps, maybe, a couple of thousand?'

'Oh dear boy, I hardly . . .' The elegant figure wriggled in cultured merriment, 'I was merely thinking of something you could knock up on a wet afternoon – for a figure of a couple of hundred guineas or so.'

The subject was dropped at once. I was itching to ask him what sort of 'proposal' was in the air between Brachan and Terby, but assumed I was about to be shown the door, and made as if to get up. I resisted the temptation to tell the sort of thing I preferred knocking up on wet afternoons.

He waved a hand which, to be honest, was none too effete. 'Stay where you are, dear boy. I'm in no hurry. Are you?'

Of course I bloody wasn't, but I didn't quite know what to say next. There are occasions when we know who's leading the conversation and there's not much we can do about it. For one thing, these fellows in high places never listen to you – even when they try out their ideas on you, they judge your reaction entirely by your facial expression. Brachan looked straight at me with the sort of piercing glance I had previously only read about in detective novels. He did this for several minutes. Then to my surprise he said: 'We need to make our society more egalitarian, don't you think?'

'Well, yes, I suppose we do.'

'For a start we ought to abolish the public schools.'

'Eh, er, um, well.'

'Then death duties ought to be made compulsory.'

'Yes, I dare say . . .'

He rattled on. For a former Tory minister it wasn't a bad programme. Certainly more radical than anything I'd ever heard the Labour Party produce at that time.

I was wondering whether I ought to insinuate the topical subject of company mergers in general and Terby's operations in particular. He did it for me.

'. . . take my job. I sit here, getting paid a fortune, apparently surrounded by some mystique that I have certainly never detected myself.'

I was dying to get out my notepad and take this down, but that would probably have stopped him in full flow. (I'm a great believer in Heisenberg's Principle.) However, the lack of opportunity to take notes concentrates the mind wonderfully, and we probably end up with greater retention than if we take fast notes we later can't decipher. Or so I like to kid myself. One thing I stress is that old Brachan certainly gave out vibrations denoting the need for confidentiality across the empty desk. He just knew I wasn't going to rush off and shove this straight into the *Jet* in a sensational way. But he wouldn't mind it coming out indirectly like this, some years later, I'm sure – such was the understanding we established at that meeting.

'. . . mergers, for example. Advising on them is one of our main sources of income in this bank, but I never know whether they're going to work. I think, looking back, that a vast majority we've been involved with have been unnecessary – not to say counterproductive; a word, incidentally, I abhor.'

'. . . one sees these young men, making their fortunes by manipulating spiv companies, and emitting a lot of cant about how they are helping to change the face of British industry . . .'

I found it difficult at this point to resist mentioning names. He continued: '. . . I'm in touch with one of these chaps at the moment. I suppose we'll do business with him – we'll have to: the City is changing, and these fellows are taking over. I expect I shall be putting him in contact with one of our clients, but I don't like it awfully much. I don't like it at all.'

8

There was a vogue word in financial circles in those days called 'synergy', meant to denote the extra benefits accruing to all concerned from the merging of two companies: two and two make five, was the way it was meant to happen. Personally I always preferred the word lethargy to describe these mergers, but throughout my time on the *Jet* I was never able to work it into a story.

I'm reminded of this because after eventually being dismissed from Lord Brachan's charming presence, I had a pretty boring afternoon, thumbing through a stockbroker's circular to see if there was anything in it for the *Jet*. The circular in question was full of the term synergy to describe the mergers it was proposing – in the hope that the share prices concerned would go up, not out of any long-term interest in British industry, you can be sure. I should have mentioned that spivvery in the City starts at the top, and that the reason these guys send their circulars to the press is that they've already stuffed their own pockets and those of their clients with the shares they are officially recommending; they want the press to get the small man in as a buyer, so that they can secure a nice profit. With ethics like that, who needs a professional code of conduct?

Why do I mention this synergy business now? Because I wasn't really studying this punk stockbrokers' circular at all. I was putting two and two together pretty fast, and that afternoon they were making five, if not six or seven.

I knew – *we* knew, Starling Cordoba and I – that the Terby/Cordoba outfit was in touch with Brachan. Brachan himself had volunteered that a wheeler-dealer was in communication with

Blizzards. At the time I'm speaking of there were several of these characters like Terby polluting the air, and Brachan could possibly have been talking about somebody else.

That morning Tring had told us we weren't 'getting around the market enough and keeping in touch with all these brokers'. He did this periodically, and this gave us – Spick and me – the perfect opportunity to wander out mid-afternoon for half an hour or so and have a cup of tea in Joe Lyons. Spick was looking pretty jaded after his weekend in Paris with Lindy – on several counts. Apart from plenty of you know what, Spick had insisted on packing in frequent visits to Lapérouse, the Tour d'Argent and other choice entries from Michelin, no doubt working on the revolution all the while.

I told Spick my suspicions over the tea-leaves.

'Well, what are you going to do about it? Find out more, or shove it into the "Walls have ears" column?'

The 'Walls have ears' column was a collection of snippets Tring ran on his page, into which all sorts of half-baked rumours found their way – about the level of ICI's forthcoming profit figures, or the chances of GEC and Thorn merging: you've read the stuff. One could already envisage a fairly innocuous paragraph on the lines 'Those in the know tell me Derek Terby is about to fix a major deal through Blizzards' – hardly worth the paper it was written on, but if something happened Tring would convince himself that it justified the banner headline 'I told you so', and the people in the Fleet Street office wouldn't understand, but credit Tring with yet another bogus scoop.

'No, let's face it. It's worth trying to do more on this. Blizzards only have very large and distinguished clients on the whole. It could be a bloody good story.'

We caught each other's eyes at that point, and pissed ourselves with embarrassed laughter, going through the sort of shared, fatuous gestures that people who've known one another for years tend to indulge in. The thought of getting a good story about the next step in our pet hate's ride to fame and ill-gotten fortune was just too much.

Spick was the first to break the noisy silence. 'There could be one quick way of finding out. Why don't you ring Terby and ask him?'

He wasn't serious. Imagine it. The embarrassment of being told where to get off by Terby. I could just hear him saying it: 'Such matters are confidential. It wouldn't be right for me to talk to a member of the financial press – even an old school friend – before informing the shareholders.'

Now, as I said, Spick had actually kept in touch with Terby for a few years after school – ironically, it started because Terby was lonely and unhappy in the accountant's office he'd entered, and Spick was working just round the corner; it was actually a case of Terby's wanting to keep in touch with *him*.

But those days were gone. Neither Spick nor I was very keen on entering the humiliation stakes with Terby at this juncture in our singularly undistinguished careers.

We dropped the subject after this inconclusive discussion, and dawdled back to the office. The Saturday morning's page was already filled, so I occupied myself thumbing through the Extel and Moodie cards – convenient summaries of company information without which the entire City of London would have been lost. I also looked at the file on Blizzards, and this way was able to assemble a list of their top clients, one of which would presumably be involved in the deal with Terby.

There are various things the dutiful financial journalist in search of a scoop can do at this stage. He can get in touch – either by telephone or over lunch – with any friends or contacts he may have in the companies he's interested in, or in the merchant banks which advise them. And if he doesn't know a soul, he can laboriously ring the directors listed on the card, one by one, and try and trap them into an indiscretion. But those guys are no fools. Nine times out of ten during my early days I used to find that what I thought was trapping them into an indiscretion was in fact a case of *their* using me. Then there are the less scrupulous professionals – accountants and solicitors – who may let slip something before or after their Sybaritic throats have been oiled with claret. And the stockbrokers, who in those lush days would let anything slip except their fat commission.

Now for a confession. Having drawn up my short list, I just couldn't be bothered to go on. The deadline business really gets you in daily journalism, and with the production lines under control for that evening I was suddenly afflicted with an attack of journalistic torpor – characterised by an inability to pick up the telephone and actually ask a question, especially on a Friday afternoon.

So I dropped it for the evening, and found myself propelled by basic instincts beyond my control into Birches, where five pints of best bitter were consumed between five-thirty and seven, among a congenial gathering of fellow torpor-sufferers. Similiar instincts took me to the telephone at this point, but Mrs Cordoba did not sound too keen on their propelling me any further in her direction, pointing out that her husband was due to make a rare visit to the family home.

When one is single in London one always feels the need to do something in the evening – not necessarily sex either: as Wintergreen once pointed out, the occasions for sin are fewer than you'd think from reading all this drivel about trendy London. A few phone calls to other girl friends produced nothing, so off I drifted to my Canonbury Square flat, all set for an evening of Mozart and Vivaldi on Radio Three. In those days I was no great shakes as a cook, and on such occasions used to buy take-home curry from the Shah in North Gower Street.

At the time I lived next door to the Rogans. You could hardly miss the Rogans, there being seven of them in all and another on the way. They'd started with one daughter, then another, and by the time it came to girl number four they were all set to give up the apparently fruitless quest for a son and heir to their debts – of which, so I gathered, there were plenty. But they took the fifty-fifty chance on number five, and hey presto, it was a son. But wait a minute. Who should one hear before long going around saying young Jonathan needed a brother? Mrs Rogan, no less. It will come as no surprise to you that these liberal people were very worried about the population problem, and passionately believed in birth control. In order to reduce the overdraft somewhat, Dr Rogan himself did a nice line in private patient vasectomies – what else?

They enjoyed a good boozy evening – especially during the late stages of pregnancy, when, as it were, they were confined. And that's how I found myself this particular Friday evening in the Rogans' kitchen at midnight, knocking back a pleasant Brouilly, and rashly agreeing to help them out in the absence of the au pair (also expecting) by taking some of the kids to school the following Monday, when Mrs Rogan had to go to the dentist.

9

A psychiatrist friend of mine reckons that forty per cent of the time we're depressed, forty per cent of the time we're okay and the other twenty per cent of the time we don't know what we feel like. I've always made it a practice in life not to decide on any course of action dreamed up in one of these states, until I've thought about it when I'm in one of the others: taking a sort of second opinion from myself, you might say.

That evening on the Brouilly became a weekend on the Brouilly, and I woke up a bit depressed, wondering just where my socialist ideals were getting me – if, indeed, they still existed. As I crossed Canonbury Square taking the Rogan kids to school, I contrasted the exquisite Georgian terraces and the gardens with the grotesque main road which bisects it – no less than the artery to the north, continually blocked by your huge container lorries, whose drivers regard traffic lights as anachronisms to which they must pay no heed, and pedestrians as targets for poisonous fumes, which with an extra bit of revving on their traffic-jammed accelerators, they can get up to quite an intolerable level. It was a matter of months, it seemed to me, before they'd be banning the pedestrian altogether, and confirming that the best Georgian Squares in London were now lorry-precincts.

Well, we're not always as logical as we'd like to think, and the whole socialist and environmental scene was a bit confused in my mind this fuzzy morning. I made a mental note, in accordance with my practice, to reconsider the position when I felt more elated, but basically I thought fuck it, it was time for me to opt out. But opting out meant the quest for independent means. Let's remember Mrs Cordoba's advice, that one should make one's pile first, as a prerequisite of putting the world to rights.

What did this mean? It meant that if my second opinion confirmed it, I was going to be forced by a gut feeling inside me to give up trying to beat them, and to join them instead. I regarded a fair proportion of the City – the proportion my work brought me into contact with – as a collection of high-class con-men with Lord Thomson's famous licence to print money. From now on I too was going to play the market, and not to be too scrupulous about it either. God knew, one got enough confidential information in the *Jet* office just that much earlier than everybody else. The City police? The Takeover Panel? Those guys were a hundred years behind the times at this stage. Once in five years the odd scandal was unearthed, but basically law or ethics enforcement was nil, and ninety-nine point nine of your Augustus Trings, Lord Brachans and their ilk were coining it. Why not me too? Make enough cash to keep the Canonbury Square flat as a London base, but go off away from the fumes and the noise to some dream hideout in the Dordogne or Auvergne, complete with knife, fork and Mrs Cordoba or her successor. Why not indeed? Then, if the fancy took me, I could enter the worlds of charity, socialism and good works when tired of the Dordogne.

My ruminations on this subject were interrupted. As I threaded my nervous way back across the road at the Canonbury Square traffic lights – sure enough, a long Continental lorry was blocking the middle of the crossroads : one of these days we'll have to walk under the bloody things – I heard loud hooting. Nothing unusual in these crazy times, and I took it that it was the usual motorist manifesting his disapproval that a fellow traveller was actually moving. But the hooting persisted, and I realised – with that sixth sense we develop when we are being driven deaf – that it was aimed at me.

The window of a Mercedes was wound down, and a peaked cap poked its way out.

' 'Allo, Tarquin, what're *you* doin' up so bright an' early?'

It was Larry, chauffeur to Augustus Tring, my boss. It may

surprise you to learn that a mere journalist should have a chauffeur, but Tring was no ordinary journalist. Having arrived at the *Jet* office by the time-honoured British route of a youth spent in Berlin and a few years in Vienna, Tring (né Trinski) had decided that the editorship of the financial page was merely a stepping stone to multifarious directorships, the City establishment, and the House of Lords. Anybody who crossed his path in those days will tell you that they too were regarded as stepping stones, no more and no less, and that chauffeur-driven car was seen by Tring as a natural way of demonstrating his style to the contacts in the banking and financial world from whom, one day, Tring was expecting an offer of a plum job.

You had to hand it to Tring. Try as I would, I couldn't help admiring him. He had arrived in the City ten years earlier, and put more people's backs up than anyone before or since. In a grating Teutonic accent he had apparently boasted that (*a*) he was going to jazz up financial journalism and make it readable and (*b*) squeeze every penny and perk out of the job that he could. Tring may have been escaping from the jackboots when he arrived in London, but he kept a pair of his own, and woe betide the loiterers in his path. He had gone a fair way towards achieving his aims – although there were no directorships yet – and for added measure was generally considered good with women and so on. Moreover the rougher edges of his accent had been polished away, and he now sounded more English than the English. His victims found the combination unforgivable. But by now, through luck, some judgement and a fair amount of insensitivity, he had made his mark. And it didn't matter that at any one time half the City hated him, because at any one time the other half didn't, and people were always moving between the two halves. Tring had got into a position where he was a significant force in the market; his prophesies on shares were often self-fulfilling, because millions of readers trusted his judgement, and even those who thought they saw through him had to take his influence into account because, as they kept telling me: 'He moves the market, Tarquin.'

There are no prizes offered for guessing which shade of City opinion chauffeur Larry represented. I was always a receptive audience for Larry's grumbles about Tring, so we used to get on famously. He in turn had convinced himself that my riotous life – which, with his low wages and large family, I fancy he participated in vicariously – kept me in bed until 11 a.m. every morning, and only just in a position to attend morning conference. To keep up the image, I explained in great detail the circumstances which had led me into the middle of Canonbury Square at the crack of 9.15 a.m.

'I was gonna say,' said Larry. 'I wouldn't normally 'spec 'a see feller like you art of bed this time mornin'.'

My image duly restored in Larry's bleary eyes, I asked him what exactly *he* was doing driving south, at a time when he would normally be heading northwards to Mill Hill, to collect Tring.

'Ferkin bastit,' he said. 'Bleedin ast me tergo up early, take 'ees bleedin dawter ter the ferkin' dentist.'

An exchange of no significance? Maybe, but Larry liked to keep his punch-lines to the end.

' 'Ere, met a mate of yorn the uvver nart. Geezer corld Sarfields. Said you uster go art wiv 'ees dawter. Been fired from 'ees job 'e 'as. Guess where I met 'im? Tring's club up St James's. Know what 'e's doin' nar? Same trade as meself. Good old 'onest chaufferin'. No kiddin'. For one of them City spivs. Cunt corld Derby, Terby or summit.'

I hope you understood all that. I've tried to capture the flavour of Larry's speech, Cockneys being a dying breed and all that. Don't think I tried to put him in the vernacular out of any prejudice though – what would I be doing with prejudices about accents, me with my boring suburban sw29 twang, full of 'ums', 'ers', 'you knows', and so grating when I hear it on a taperecorder that I positively (that's a good sw29 word) twinge.

Anyway, the gist of it was that dear old Larry had met Mr Southfields, as I knew – and still know him. During my pre-Lindy Fanshawe days (that is, very pre-Mrs Cordoba), I'd had a brief affair with Judith Southfields, which ended in disaster in the corner of a wheat field near Glyndebourne. I'll spare you the details –

only to say she'd warded me off so successfully for so long, that when it came to it, it didn't – but I'd kept in touch with them until recently, if only because I enjoyed having left-right arguments with her old man over the Léoville-Barton, courtesy the profits of the firm of stockbrokers he worked for – or had worked for, if Larry's tale was correct: by now Larry had been hooted on by the rest of the traffic jam, and was speeding off towards Highbury Corner in the company of Jimmy Young.

Mr Southfields wasn't one of your corporation men, and had never been able to stand being a stockbroker anyway, having drifted into it after the war, like so many displaced naval officers. I recalled that the last time we'd failed to put the world to rights he'd been a bit worried about an impending merger with another firm. One couldn't tell with a nice guy like that whether he really wanted some commiseration for being fired, but I inclined to the view that congratulations were probably more in order. Either way, he of all people certainly wouldn't mind being pumped about his new boss. Jesus – Mr Southfields working as chauffeur for Derek ('can you pass "O" level if you get twenty per cent?') Terby? What bloody next?

10

What do you do when you want to speak to a guy's chauffeur? You can't exactly ring them up – during the day they're always too busy sitting in their Rollses and Bentleys on double yellow lines, daring the parking attendants to book them, while the likes of you and me are towed off.

I had to suppress my natural excitement about Larry's news, and meanwhile all I could do was ring Mrs Southfields and ask her what time she expected the great man to come home. Despite their change in income bracket, the Southfields were still living in one of those stockbroker villages in Sussex, I gathered. I was damned if I was going to go round to Terby's offices and hang about outside looking for his chauffeur although, granted, it would be less humiliating than looking for Terby himself.

'Why don't you come down and have some supper?' said Mrs Southfields. 'Judith's here and I'm sure she'd be delighted to see you again, Tarquin.'

I rang Mrs Cordoba – in her role as mother figure – to check whether this would be all right; she said George was still haunting the place – 'what right has my husband to spend so much time at home, Tarquin?' – but too boozed to latch onto the hints she was dropping about her interest in the Terby/Cordoba machinations with Lord Strachan.

At the conference I said nothing about my deepening suspicions on the Terby affair; Tring devoted most of the time to a story about the Chancellor of the Exchequer, whose only point was that he, Tring, had managed to have a few words with him, the Chancellor, at 'some boring Government reception'.

It was a nice June day, midway between the Derby and Wimbledon, with the strawberry season in full swing. The birds were singing – or believed to be singing outside London if you could still rely on the *Guardian*'s 'A Country Diary' – and I decided to drive down to Burwash, stopping at a nice inn for the odd pint on the way. Driving through South London, Croydon and environs was not too redolent of your Shelley or Keatsian summer's evening, but I kept my eyes closed for most of this time (metaphorically speaking of course) and turned up Mozart's fifth violin concerto loud and clear on the car wireless.

It's just possible in some of those Sussex villages to get a pint of beer which doesn't taste like Persil, and I made my contribution to the progress of humanity by asking the landlord of the Four Crosses to turn up the Muzak – which, with total bafflement on his face, he did. Then I hopped back into my Mini, and before you could say Derek Terby I was pulling up outside the Southfields' seventeenth-century cottage, complete with its beams, its albertines, and its midge bites. The only visible sign of Mr Southfields' decline in status was the Rolls outside, instead of the usual Renault 16. He explained that Terby had let him take it home because he was out of the country for a few days. 'Where? What's he up to?' I said, quick as a flash.

'Oh he's gone over to Switzerland on some shady business or other. He'll be back either tomorrow or Wednesday.'

We had a great evening. To tell the truth, I used to find as a bachelor that some – not all – of one's most pleasant relationships with girls took place after we'd got the sex bit out of the way – or not out of the way, but certainly established whether we would or we wouldn't – so that we could get down to being good friends again, as it were. The number of characters I knew in similar positions doesn't bear thinking about – having it off with somebody they couldn't stand, and preserving all these beautiful friendships with girls they'd first met at the local convent dance. Judith was in good form that evening, and the claret was pouring out of Mr Southfields' cellar. All right, I thought: the episode with Judith in the wheat fields had been a disaster, but so what? She with her flaxen hair and blue eyes – an Irish way of describing a girl of Irish extraction – was still totally devastating. We'd got nowhere – physically – in three years, but mentally we were right on each others' wavelength (Radio Iceland). Maybe it was a question of waiting just another three years. By the end of the evening I was also thinking how attractive Mrs Southfields looked at the tender age of fifty-five or so – a bull point for Judith's chances in years to come. Anyway, Judith went up to bed, and Mr Southfields offered me some of his malt whisky to round off the evening and get down to the serious business of the meeting.

'Now, Tarquin, I expect you want to talk about Terby,' he said.

'Well, er, yes, it hadn't been completely off my agenda,' I confessed.

Mr Southfields downed his single malt, reached for the bottle, and poured himself another. I must say, these guys who manage to reach their fifties without being either corpulent or cadaverous (I must watch the alliteration) always look very impressive. I know it's all to do with your metabolic rate and so on, but the lean and hungry look with plenty of hair on top at that age – greying gracefully of course – is something I'd happily aspire to. They succeed in bridging the gap with the younger generation without actually falling into the chasm of demeaning trendiness (careful Tarquin).

Magnanimity was now oozing out of him; the sweeping gesture he made as yet again he refilled his glass implied that I could not only top up my own – he being too sozzled to move anything but his right arm – but could help myself to anything I fancied, including Judith and the wine cellar – in that order no doubt.

'The thing is, Tarquin, these fellows are so indiscreet.' (More, more.)

'. . . you know I've been getting far more information since I became Terby's chauffeur than I ever came across while stock-broking.'

'Yes I'm sure,' I said encouragingly. We were in the home straight now. My main problem – he reached for the Glenlivet again – would be to prevent him from falling asleep at the last fence.

'Take this latest deal of his. The other day he had lunch with Lord Brachan in the Carlton Club. You can imagine the scene: the grammar school king of the share-tipping columns – God to the *Sunday Times* Business News and the secondary figures in the City, but spittle to Brachan – fumbling his way across the Grand Tory carpet and being deliberately introduced by Brachan to people he knew would say, "Terby? Terby? No don't believe I . . ." '

Boy, could I imagine it. And with relish. Terby, his first time in the Carlton Club, ordering pheasant and burgundy, Brachan with total disdain saying, 'I think I'll have liver and bacon and a glass of Guinness please.'

Mr Southfields continued. 'You see, Tarquin. These people are simply amazing. Brachan will go to great lengths to see that his office isn't bugged – that other bank having been caught napping a few years ago – but he's so used to playing the arrogant aristocratic role expected of him that it never occurs to him to lower his voice when I'm around.'

I was getting worried about all these deviations from the main point. Mr Southfields' right arm had already made several further deviations around the Glenlivet. 'You were saying about this deal?'

'Oh yes. Now where was I? Yes. They left the Club and Brachan's chauffeur was late. He was in a hurry for his next appointment, so my considerate new boss, Mister Derek Terby, offered him a lift.'

'Go on.'

'Hang on, just wanna have a pee.'

Well, you can imagine how I felt at this stage. Here was Mr Southfields on the verge of giving me the great scoop, to say nothing of the chance to make a real killing. Let's face it. I'd been thinking over my attitude to what *I* could make out of this with advance knowledge, on the way down in the car – thereby demonstrating to you my belief in re-examining one's major decisions in the light of changing moods. While I was driving through outer Sussex, the sheer sordidness of my so-called career as a share-tipping financial journalist was vibrating through my brain loud and clear. The logical progression to a job with some City broking outfit was even more repugnant.

Now we all get the opting out feeling occasionally, but unless I wanted to live on national assistance I would definitely have to dabble in the market myself to finance what those fellows in Throgmorton Street would no doubt call my opting position. There was a great euphemism that Spick was using in his share market reports at the time – the phrase 'good buying' to explain an outrageously rapid increase in a share price as a result of guys acting on inside information. It was abundantly clear to me that if I was going not only to buy but also to live in my dream cottage in the Dordogne, then Tarquin would have to do a lot of good buying. My political beliefs? We may return to those later. On the other hand, we may not.

Now if Mr Southfields' information on this Terby deal was good enough with any luck I could do all my 'good buying' at once, and it would be a case of 'Dordogne, here we come'. Earlier in the evening Mr Southfields – who incidentally, while these reflections were going on was still in the lavatory: had he no sense of priorities? – had admitted that he'd been hoping all along to get the boot from his stockbroker's office, and that he wanted no sympathy on that score. I'd always known he was a square peg in that particular bed of nails and now it was confirmed that he was something of an opter-out himself. His son, Judith's brother, had confused the issue, perversely dropping in again after a few years on the Afghan trail, to join the firm which had just fired his father.

Redundancy and compensation payments are particularly welcome to those who are dying to leave a place anyway, and so it was with Mr Southfields. He took the chauffeuring job after hearing from somebody in the local village pub about some firm – started by recently failed Oxbridge men of course, the flower of our nation – which was trying, in its own words, 'to upgrade the chauffeuring market'. (The things education can do for you, but then I suppose I'm the last one to talk.) Apart from enabling him to have a good laugh embarrassing his former colleagues when he met them, cap in hand, around Throgmorton Street, the job also established him in a low income bracket for the rest of the fiscal year, thereby qualifying him for huge tax rebates. Mr Southfields had thought of opening a pub, but didn't fancy the hours – 'Much better open an antique shop next door to a pub, Tarquin, and shove the closed sign up whenever one feels like it.'

I trust this doesn't slow down the pace of my account too much. I must sound like a commentator filling in time while rain has stopped play – which in a sense was true. But I want wherever possible to give you the flavour of things, without going into all those boring descriptions of every item of furniture (human and otherwise) which are de rigueur in what passes for writing nowadays.

I was beginning to think Mr Southfields had fallen asleep in the loo, when he reappeared. My feeling that he was now looking very much the worse for wear was confirmed too quickly for my liking: he forgot the steps leading from the hall into the low-ceilinged cottage drawing room, and crashed his head on one of those oak beams which reassure us on such occasions that we're still in the Home Counties. It was evident at this stage that Terby was not the name which was most on his mind. 'Christ Almighty,' he bellowed, and my hero gave a lifelike imitation of a bear with a sore head as he groped his way to a chair, all the while moaning rhetorical questions about why the hell he'd bought a house designed for Tudor pygmies in the first place.

'Brain cells,' he muttered. 'How many brain cells do I lose every time I bash my head on that thing?' This, again, was rhetorical I thought. But I made reassuring noises and suggested that perhaps he had better go up to bed.

I led him up the stairs – the secret of Terby's dealings still unrevealed – and steered him towards his room. I think he was aware that as a result of his conduct I felt I was missing out on something, but any attempts of his to rectify the situation were lost on me. As we staggered together along the upstairs passage, he several times muttered the phrase 'railway trains, railway trains,' without further clarification.

I was relieved to find that the Southfields, at their tender stage in life, still shared a bed. Many couples of my acquaintance live in separate rooms, not to say separate countries, by their fifties. I raised Mr Southfields onto his side of the matrimonial shrine by simple mechanics – that is, I got him as far as the bed in a sort of standing-up position, and let him fall onto it, taking care to raise later whatever part of his body failed to make it first time, in this case his right leg, as he lay there flat out and prone. Unfortunately, my alcohol-oppressed brain overestimated the leverage which would be required to effect this last stage, and Mr Southfields rolled over too far, landing four square on Mrs Southfields. This wouldn't have been too bad if Mrs Southfields hadn't at this stage pushed him gently aside, muttering good-humouredly – and still in her sleep – 'Stop it, Tarquin. Not here.'

Fortunately Mr Southfields didn't hear this remark, and I myself was not going to bring it up again. I've always thought that our dreams are confused enough already, without extra help from Freudians, anti-Freudians and the rest. Nevertheless, it set me thinking, and as I walked back along the corridor towards my own quarters (Mr Southfields still liked to throw in the odd nautical term), I hesitated as I passed Judith's own room. Should I look in? Just a peep, perhaps. One always seems to get the urge in other people's houses. Why not lay (forgive me) the ghost of that episode in the hayfields near Glyndebourne I told you about?

I tiptoed in and gave her a peck on the lips. Just testing, you might say. She smiled unconsciously, stretching her arms up in an inviting manner. It was a hot night – you could say that again, at this stage of my base desires – and her bedclothes were only half on. The effect of stretching her arms upwards was to displace her nightie in the lower reaches, thereby giving me a full snapshot of things I hoped were to come. My hand moved irresistibly towards its next resting place, risking the old army rebuke for unwarranted speed: 'Manners: tits first.' But it wasn't just hastiness which made the umpire cry fault on this occasion. Oh, no.

Like mother, like daughter, out came the considered judgement:
'Stop it, Tarquin. Not here.' An answer, however, which at least
allowed for the interpretation: 'But somewhere else.' Not an un-
profitable evening, viewed in the medium term, provided that Mr
Southfields coughed up on the morrow. I slept like a log, and
dreamt of the Dordogne.

II

You hear of these guys who are fit as a fiddle after a night on the booze, but I have yet to meet them. Mr Southfields looked none too steady at breakfast, and I own to having felt about five below par myself. However, a few gallons of unsweetened Jaffa juice helped, and I reminded my host of the original agenda. 'You were saying about Terby . . . ?'

'Terby? Terby? Oh yes, Terby. Well, he's getting very sensitive to criticism, you know. Like all these fellows, the one thing he doesn't like to hear is the truth. Having had a good run with all that sycophantic crap in the business pages, he's even got the bloody Tories criticising him for being just a share manipulator.'

'When they were out of office they reckoned he was helping to change the face of British industry.'

'Yes, well the only face he's helped to change is his bloody own, and he knows it. Now that they've decided the capitalist system only worked when they were in opposition, this lot have got their claws into him.'

Good stuff, but still vague on detail, I thought. Time was running out and I had to drive up to the office. 'So what's he up to?' I said.

'Up to? He's trying to become respectable, and he's trying to do so fast.'

'Was there something about a merger?'

'Yes, he's decided it's the only way out – or in, I should say. What's more Brachan, who personifies the sort of responsibility Terby wants to attain, is also desperate for this to go through.'

'What? Why? I should have thought Brachan would have

grave reservations myself.'

'The City's changing, the Americans are moving in, the old-fashioned places like Blizzards are losing their esteem. The Yanks tend to drop in to admire his lordship and his decanters, then take their business elsewhere, pinching some of Blizzards' clients en route.'

'So Blizzards is declining like everything else in this country. But where does Terby fit into it? I should have thought he was the last person they want.'

'Well, after suddenly emerging as ordinary mortals – who like ordinary mortals can cock things up – Blizzards are desperate for a big success.'

'Arranging a *Terby* merger?' Scorn registered in my voice as I pronounced the dreaded name, with the maximum of contempt thrown into the first syllable.

'Come, come Tarquin. Consider the aesthetic beauty of a scheme under which Terby would gain respectability and Blizzards recover something of their lost reputation by engineering the whole thing. The harlots of the financial press – oh sorry, Tarquin – will be falling over themselves with unctuous exclusive pieces about how Brachan "masterminded" the deal.'

'No doubt gaining or recovering respectability won't leave them short of cash.'

'My dear Tarquin. If this thing goes through the way they're planning it, Terby's move into respectability will give him at one fell swoop far more money than he's ever made out of most of his shady deals.'

'Mr Southfields, do you mind my asking which is the company involved?'

'I don't mind your asking, but I can't help you on that one. I wish I knew. *That* Tarquin, is what we've got to find out if we're going to get our just rewards out of this business.'

'You said Terby comes back Wednesday?'

'Yes, that's tomorrow. Then I can resume my eavesdropping. Meanwhile, all I can tell you is that it's what they call a "reverse takeover", with one of the biggest UK industrial companies bidding for Terby Holdings, the idea being that Big Derek will run the merged concern, and the present managing director of whatever it is will be kicked upstairs to be life president.'

'That's all very well, but where does it get us? The thing we really need now is the name of the other company.'

'You're the financial journalist around here, Tarquin. Over to you. Now you've got a God-given chance to prove yourself.'

'Didn't they give away any clues at all during this otherwise delightfully indiscreet car ride?'

'Not really. Unless . . . unless.'

'Unless what?'

'Well there *was* something. Not very much. Our Derek, showing a sensitivity I hadn't credited him with before, actually voiced some concern about how the deposed managing director would take it all.'

'For God's sake. Who the hell is it? He *must* want to become reputable. But how does this amazing display of humane feelings help us?'

'Only that Brachan said, "Oh that's no problem. He'll have more time to devote to his railway trains".'

Mr Southfields' face took on a pained expression. 'I suppose there isn't any more of that orange juice darling?'

The Southfields' house being the sort of place where everybody did their own thing – Mrs Southfields had discovered women's lib while Germaine Greer was in nappies – this request for service struck me as a sign that the old man really wasn't up to further discussions at this stage. I thanked them all for everything, mentally regretting the omissions of the night before, and set off for the office. Judith accompanied me down the garden path, looking pretty fetching in the Primavera colours which went rather well with her pale complexion. There was a hint of your classical nude in her figure – Rubens and predecessors – which did not accord with the straight up and down model female of our times. I suppose it is the modern conditioning process which allows the Mrs Cordobas to get away with it, but if you conducted an opinion poll of all males from 55 BC to the present day I know who'd get the 'more than fifty per cent'. Judith Southfields every time.

However, there was one thing I *couldn't* get from Judith South-fields at the time, and as I drove back via Tunbridge Wells and Sevenoaks I saw Mrs Cordoba's wicked thin-lipped smile behind every traffic jam. What was more, I must find out whether she'd got any more out of husband George on the Terby business.

I left the Mini in the underground car park at London Wall, thinking the Harry Lime type scene under there was an appropriate background to a day on which I hoped to embark on my life of financial crime. At the office I found that Augustus Tring had taken the day off to go to some merchant banker's box at the races, and that his deputy was in charge. This was equivalent to us all having a day off, so I dived to the phone and rang my little Starling.

'Tarquin, my pet,' she purred. 'It seems ages.'

'How about lunch?'

'No darling, I can't make lunch. I've got a school managers' meeting. How about this evening? There's some steak here – or we could go to Le Français? Drop in after work.'

'Okay. Any news about Terby?'

'Darling, I can't talk over the phone. My telephone may be tapped. See you this evening,' she cooed.

Jesus, what was that? Telephones being tapped? Everybody I know thinks his telephone's being tapped, but it's usually some poor mother from Lewisham dialling in to try and get through to her daughter in Letchworth. However, one must let Mrs Cordoba have her illusions.

I looked around the office. With Tring away, most of them had disappeared to Birches even earlier than usual – it was only ten past eleven. The office boys were sorting out the files in desultory fashion: they always showed more enthusiasm later in the day for the Stock Exchange price list, in which one felt they had a personal interest. One of my colleagues was doing his Australian pools, and another his expenses. In a corner Jack Spick was typing furiously away. I asked him what the hurry was: imminence of revolution?

'Oh it's just a routine press release I'm doing for the Irish workers on the Barbican site. There's a huge demonstration down there at the moment.'

'I must say, I didn't notice it when I parked my car.'

'Well, I say huge, but I mean we're hoping it'll build up.'

'Unlike the Barbican,' I muttered.

Over his shoulder I caught a glimpse of the words 'Capitalist oppression which only a real mass-based workers' revolution can . . .' I left him to work on wrecking the system, and concentrated on my new plans to make the present system work for me.

12

Railway trains, railway trains. My only clue. Brachan had told Terby that the deposed managing director of the other company would have more time to devote to his railway trains. The phrase 'his railways trains' could be a sardonic reference to big trains of the sort we ride in; or, more likely I thought, the man was one of these cranks who never grow out of the Hornby toy set stage, and had model gauge railways all over his house. Probably spent too much time on them already, which was why they wanted to remove him.

What to do? I idly thumbed through the telephone directory. There was a Model Railway Manufacturing Company in York Way, N1 – conveniently near Kings Cross and St Pancras. Automatic response, get hold of a list of the directors. Catch: who was I looking for anyway? There were various model railway magazines listed, and there must be clubs all over the place. Jesus, what a laborious process.

No this was the wrong way round. I knew the other company was one of the country's biggest industrial companies. The man concerned was managing director. You sometimes get joint-managing directors, but usually there's only one. It must be in the top fifty at the very least.

The first thing to do was get out the files, leave out the obviously unlikely candidates and compile a list of possibilities. I did this, assuming that companies like Shell, Unilever, Esso and GEC had hardly reached the stage where they needed somebody like Terby to sort them out. If they were kicking somebody like Weinstock out, we might as well *all* resign. This process of selection narrowed the list to about twenty companies, not such a daunting task.

I then got out the Extel cards I referred to earlier, and made a list of all the managing directors of the companies concerned. On such occasions it's amazing what you can do from the filing system, without even so much as picking up the telephone. In particular, newspaper offices have a bible in the shape of a fat volume which lists most British companies and their directors.

Before lunch I went through all the companies I could think of or find which were remotely connected with railways – including those strange nineteenth-century companies based in London with railways in South America. As I had suspected, there was no link between the names on my list and any of these companies – from British Rail onwards.

Neither Spick nor I had any lunch appointments, and at about twelve-thirty we drifted out to Birches for a beer. I overheard one of those braying stockbrokers saying that Terby Holdings had gone up 3p and he thought there wasn't much time to waste. Perhaps the 'good buying' had begun already. But I'm not a great one for working on an empty stomach – in which category I include a sandwich lunch – and I readily succumbed to Spick's suggestion that we should wander down to Cheapside and grab a bite in the upstairs part of the Poulbot. We bumped into a couple of characters from the *Financial Times*, and washed the Entrecôte Béarnaise down with a few carafes.

We wandered back at about three, and I got going on the next stage of my search: my favourite book: *Who's Who*. Boy, if they ever invite me onto Desert Island Discs, *Who's Who* is the book *I'll* be taking along with my Mozart, my Vivaldi, my Monteverdi and my Delius. I decided to thumb through the entries for all the managing directors of the various companies on my short list, in the hope of finding some sort of clue, there being no question that all these guys would be included, complete with their dates of birth, their education, their main directorships and their hobbies. Their *hobbies*.

Honestly, if you believed some of those entries you'd think the entire country spent its time playing bridge in the garden. The truth is, most of those businessmen are so busy flogging their guts out that their main hobby is sleeping in an armchair in front of the television. But they never admit that on their *Who's Who* form.

I whipped through their entries, just looking for the listed hobbies. Apart from the bridge and the gardening, there was the bridge and the gardening and the gardening and the bridge. Are you expecting me to say I got to the twentieth without any luck, and then by the strangest of coincidences happened to meet the guy later in the evening at Le Français, talking simultaneously about his work and his hobby, just to give me that extra clue? Sorry folks. This is no detective story. Sometimes in life things actually happen quite quickly, the way you want them. At my seventeenth entry – Allan, Henry – I found just what I was looking for. There it was, leaping out of the small print: 'Hobbies: small gauge railways'.

Well, this was my moment of truth. The pieces of information from Mrs Cordoba, Lord Brachan and Mr Southfields fitted together neatly. The Amalgamated Industrial Company – generally known as AIC – managing director Mr Henry Allan, CBE, was on the verge of bidding for Terby Holdings. Allan was going to be ousted from his seat and Terby would be crowned king of an industrial company: an *industrial* company: real live industry, manufacturing goods and not pieces of financial paper.

Pausing for reflection, I glanced over the shoulder of Jack Spick, who was sitting next to me. There he was, hacking out a comment on the dip in profits just announced by one of the biggest building contractors. I caught a glimpse of the words '. . . the main reason for the contraction in profits was obviously the hold-ups on the Barbican site: it is to be hoped that the company can bring its labour relations under better control in the coming year . . .' Oh Spick, where is thy Span?

All right though, Spick's position in this day and age was pretty schizophrenic. But what about mine? No, there could be no question of a change of mind. I'd decided to postpone my triumphal entry into charity, socialism and good works at least until I'd made my pile, and I could quote you plenty of examples in the House of Commons today. I had the information. I must act. My stockbroking contacts had used me often enough, pushing their lousy share tips into the paper on a slow news day. Now I must use them.

What I'm getting at is that however useless for all concerned these mergers used to prove in the long run, there were always great profits to be had in the short term.

To get the shareholders to move out of their characteristic state of total inertia in those days they had to be bribed. This meant that the price offered by the bidding company for the shares of the firm to be taken over was usually well above the existing market value, the difference being justified by all sorts of claptrap about the future growth of profits as a result of the merger. Remember all that synergy rubbish I mentioned earlier.

Now at the time I'm talking of, the 1960s and early 1970s, some of the more unscrupulous financial journalists used to be up to their necks in the shares they were writing about, and oh boy, was Tring quick on the blower to his own brokers whenever he heard that the reporter in our office who specialised on North Sea oil was writing about some firm with a new discovery. I'd hate to say dabbling in shares warped a journalist's judgement, but do you think all those guys would have been tipping the Rolls Razor and English and Overseas shares at their peak in the sixties if they hadn't been swimming in them? Everybody seemed to know John Bloom was about to crash except the experts who were advising us.

The truth is I'd been boring my publishing friends for years with suggestions that Paul Ferris on the City was a bit dated and that they wanted to go for the corruption angle, when lo and behold, the corruption angle – the unacceptable face of capitalism etc – was in front of our very eyes and me still planning the book over the pints of Worthington which kept me from my typewriter. But now we had the Takeover Panel and the government hot on the trail, trying to practise the controls and ethics which I'd been preaching. Even while I sat there reflecting, there landed on my desk a copy of a speech by the Minister for Trade and Industry saying financial journalists would be included in the list of those with privileged information whose share dealings would in future have to be restricted by law. True, representatives of the Stock Exchange were standing up making speeches in which they said statutory controls of inside dealings were impossible, and you'd have to rely on 'codes' and a man's word being his bond. But the message coming across loud and clear at four o'clock that sunny June afternoon was that the sands were running out.

It was still not only possible but not even illegal to act on inside information. 'Buy now, Tarquin, or forever adhere to your principles. But whatever you do, don't be the first victim of the sort of policing controls you've been advocating yourself.'

I made a quick call to Mr Southfields, to let him know the important clue about Henry Allan I'd picked up.

'You're sure the deal is on, are you?' I asked. 'No last minute hitches or anything?'

'Absolutely sure. Terby rang me from Zurich just now to say could I meet him at London Airport tonight and take him straight to Blizzards to see Lord Brachan. He said it was vital. He had to sign some document before it went off to the printer. There's only one deal which could bring Terby and Blizzards together like that.'

13

Your average financial journalist can take in quite a lot of liquor – he has to: press receptions may be a daily routine for him, but they're an annual occasion for his hosts, who like everybody to get smashed with them. My collegue Jim Parsons had taken advantage of Tring's absence to indulge himself even more than usual over a four-hour lunch in the George and Vulture, with the result that he was in no state to do the stock market report that afternoon. I readily volunteered myself as a replacement, because this gave me a perfect opportunity to talk round the market about Terby Holdings without arousing any suspicions.

All you do with the market report on the Financial Page is say which shares have gone up or down most, and why. If you can't find out why, you just make it up. I established conclusively that there was in fact precious little going on in Terby Holdings at the moment – a 3p rise in price that morning had been followed by a 3p drop in the afternoon. In the City of London stockbrokers can buy or sell shares for you, but most of the business goes via a central pool of 'jobbers' (originally 'stockjobbers'). The jobbers are wholesalers; there are only a few for any one stock, and oh boy did they mark up the price of a share when they got a whiff of the sort of information *I* had. On this occasion I telephoned the key dealers, and dropped in on some of them – making sure that my probing questions about Terby Holdings were buried in probing questions about everything else. They just thought I was an over-enthusiastic newcomer, and smelled nothing unusual.

Having satisfied myself that there was nothing going on, I rang up almost every stockbroking contact I had, and arranged to meet them individually at assorted bars around the City during the next two days. I then typed out the market report – making no reference whatsoever to Terby Holdings – had a quick pint in Birches with Spick, and drove up to St Johns Wood.

I wasn't wearing my spectacles as I stood waiting for Mrs Cordoba's door to open – not out of vanity, but because they were pinching my ears and needed to be adjusted. I *thought* my Starling was looking rather young, and then on closer inspection saw it was her 'step-daughter' who had opened the door.

Mrs Cordoba was on the upstairs terrace, drinking Pimms. 'Sweetheart, be a dear and finish this for me. We must be quick. George is bringing his new girl friend here yet again to see the children.'

We drove to Le Français in Fulham Road via the Anglesea in Selwood Terrace – a pleasant summer pub where you can stand outside if the pollen count isn't too high. I wasn't intending to divulge too much of the information I'd got from Mr Southfields, so I had to go easy on the drink.

At the restaurant we had a French regional duck dish whose name I forget, other than that it wasn't à l'Orange, from which you can count me out any time. We talked mainly about sex and Catholicism, but towards the end Mrs Cordoba became rather journalistic, and started probing.

'What have I found out? Nothing much,' I said.

Her thin lips got thinner, and her face assumed the wizened, somewhat witchlike expression which I suppose was meant to be a grin. I always found this devastatingly sexy and I sensed that we were in for what economists call a 'trade off' – in this case between information and sex.

'Come home, Tarquin. I *know* you found out something. Otherwise you would have been pumping me to see if I'd got anything out of George.'

'What rubbish,' I said with total unconviction. Let's face it, I've never been a match for feminine intuition.

'I think I'd better go home,' she said after a pause.

'Oh, I was thinking we might go back to my flat.'

She grinned again, even more wickedly. 'I'm sure we can come to an arrangement.'

We drove back to my place and came to an arrangement. As I have implied before, making love to Mrs Cordoba was hardly a prolonged orgy: in sporting terms it took about as long as a quick conversion after a not too difficult try.

'Feeling better, my love?'

I'll say I was. Nor, with all the excitement of the Terby deal whirling around my head, was I experiencing any feeling of anticlimax.

'Now about Terby,' I said, mixing a large quantity of Florida Orange. 'The thing is . . .'

'I know you're hedging when you say that, Tarquin. Come on, out with it.'

'Well, look at it this way. You're right: they *are* up to something. But I don't think it'll do your shares any harm. There's no need for you to worry.'

'But I need to sell some, darling. I want the money.'

'Well, if you can, you ought to hang on a bit, because the price is bound to go up. Why do you want the money?'

She paused for at least half a minute, and looked more or less straight through me. 'Well, if you *must* know, George is behaving rather peculiarly. He's cut off some of my allowance, he's got a private detective trailing me, and he's thinking of getting a divorce.'

Plop, splash, pow. My Florida Orange saw the light of the carpet, and I reached for the hard stuff. Holy Godfathers, as Father Wintergreen used to say. Well, well. Wow, wow. Jesus. Oh Lord. My God. Ay, Ay, Ay . . .

14

Sitting there – or rather reeling on the floor – being told all this, I found my sense of horror was tinged with a certain excitement. It wasn't every day one got caught up in this sort of thing. Consider her next remark: 'Look outside, Tarquin. Is there a man watching us?'

I opened the window and leaned out cautiously. There were none of your private detectives in sight, although there was some hippie-looking guy lounging around in the middle of the square, smoking what was no doubt a reefer.

'There's nobody out there. Look, who are you trying to kid?'

Mrs Cordoba peered out of the window and waved. So private detectives come in all shapes and sizes these days. Stood to reason, I suppose, but I'd more or less assumed they still wore trilbies and mackintoshes. Who's to prove we're not all being trailed if they wander about like that?

'What the bloody hell are you up to?' I yelled insofar as one can yell at 2 a.m. in Canonbury Square without waking one of the Rogan kids. A rhetorical yell, what was more, as I continued: 'You lead me on. You come to my house. You let me get involved with private detectives. You . . .'

I saw it all. So that was what it was all about. It had been too easy the other Sunday night, being handed over to Mrs Cordoba on a plate by Lindy Fanshawe. The perfect bait. The born sucker. Part one of his affair with a married woman, and it had been a cunning plan, concocted by her lawyers beneath the rugged elms of Grays Inn.

By definition we solipsists assume we are in the centre of

events, when in fact we are on the periphery. 'What do you *mean* Tarquin my love,' said old narrow lips, stubbing out a half smoked cigarette. '*You're* not involved with private detectives. Poor dear. You don't think . . . you don't think for one moment that this is about *you* do you?'

She laughed, possibly in genuine amusement; I couldn't be sure.

'Tarquin, *I'm* the one who's involved with that gentleman down there, and *he's* no private detective.'

'Well who is he?'

Thin lips. Cruel smile this time. 'He's my lover.'

'Who the hell am I then?'

'Good point, darling. Good point. You don't think we could invite him up do you? He's very sweet. I think you'd like each other.'

I scowled and said nothing.

Mrs Cordoba took out a handkerchief and made crying motions. 'Sweetheart, I did warn you in a way. I wasn't intending to come back here. He was expecting me. He's very possessive.'

'What about the private detective? Isn't *he* possessive too? Where's he? Under that character's Afghan coat?'

She recovered herself pretty fast – if, indeed she had anything to recover from. 'You see, George didn't walk out on *me*, nor I on George. Things just happened.'

She must have guessed my analysis of the 'woman-who's-desperate-for-lovers-because-her-husband's-walked-out-on-her syndrome' which I mentioned above. *I'll* say things were just happening. I was even beginning to feel hurt and wronged now, in spite of the fact that I regarded it as a purely sexual affair, with a few laughs thrown in, not forgetting her original tip that Terby and George Cordoba were up to something. But if she'd managed to deceive me in this matter – or at least, shall we say, not to go out of her way to stop me being deceived, how could I trust her on the takeover business? Was she just playing around in that matter too? It even occurred to me that perhaps she knew a lot more than she was saying, and found my own investigations into the Terby deal an amusing diversion. For all I knew the deal was being announced the following morning: all this stuff about her not communicating with George might well be a blind – isn't it true that it's only after a marriage has failed through a breakdown in communications that couples start talking to each other?

Meanwhile, back in the Canonbury Square jungle, someone was waiting to communicate with Mrs Cordoba.

'I'm sorry Tarquin, I think I'd better go.'

I went down the stairs with her, not because I wanted to but because with the time switches in that house you could be left falling downstairs in total darkness. I drew the line at meeting the great lover, however. All I can say is he looked about seventeen and she'd probably pinched him off one of her daughters. But I couldn't help feeling humiliated by the episode – a factor which was probably in the not-too-subconscious background when I delivered my valedictory remark to the great lady: 'Be your age.'

15

After being given the brush-off by Mrs Cordoba, I needed a few diversions to concentrate my emotions. The hurt certainly lingers on such occasions, and I didn't sleep too soundly. I woke up raring to get on with my coup. This was to be my big day, whatever had happened in the Mrs Cordoba stakes. Terby would already have seen Lord Brachan and signed on the dotted line, having been picked up by Mr Southfields at London Airport the previous evening.

The most valuable words my stockbroking contacts had all said to me at one time or another were: 'Remember Tarquin, if you ever want to do any dealing through me, I'll be delighted to handle the business, big or small.' If ever I needed those old clichés like 'a man's word is his bond', I needed them now. I was about to do an awful lot of business, and I was depending on the integrity of the corrupt system I couldn't stand to help me in my hour of need. There was the added relish of realising that in this case the adage 'it's not what you know but who you know', was only part of the truth. I knew something, and I knew who to place my business with.

While I was in the shower I ran over the various possibilities. Share prices are basically a matter of supply and demand: a small demand for a share can push the price up a lot in circumstances where there aren't many on offer. On the other hand, an investment manager who goes about his business cleverly can acquire huge quantities of stock from various sources without disturbing the price too much. It takes a lot to move your ICIS, but the *Jet* office had had a beautiful ride punting on some share called

C

S. Symons in the early 1960s, when the price more or less doubled in a thin market – from two bob to four bob.

I had two problems. One was to acquire as many Terby Holdings shares as I possibly could. The other was to do so without disturbing the price. After that, splendid. Let it shoot up. It was standard practice in those carefree days to offer more than the existing market value of a share in a takeover bid; the only question was how much of a premium the Amalgamated Industrial Company, via Lord Brachan's machinations, would be putting on Terby Holdings. Once I'd done *my* buying, I could introduce the story as my scoop at conference. The rest of the office could climb on the bandwagon during the course of the day, and *Jet* readers – bless their hearts – would be informed in due course.

Unfortunately I wasn't in the happy position of a corrupt pension fund manager. Given a situation like this, the real crooks can load themselves with stock for their own personal account, and if things go wrong they merely bundle the stuff into the fund, and make their collective pensioners carry the can. If things go right, well they keep it for themselves.

The great thing in my favour though was that it was Day Three of the Stock Exchange account. It was a real case of live now and pay later in those days, because you didn't have to cough up the cash until Settlement Day, ten days after the fortnightly account closed. What I aimed to do was stuff myself with Terby's shares on the Wednesday and Thursday (Days Three and Four of the account) and write the story of the impending bid for Friday's Financial Page. Then all I needed to do was wait until the story was confirmed, and sell the shares once the share price of Terby Holdings had shot up. Get it? No money goes out from me, and I collect the difference. It's meant to be illegal to buy shares if you haven't got the money, but the Stock Exchange is full of smart operators doing things 'within the account'. Occasionally some of these characters get too greedy, and they're in trouble. Me, I was going to be very greedy, but on what I regarded as pretty good information, which would keep me well away from trouble.

After my shower I took off the bath hat which protects us long-haired individuals from contact with water, and shaved those few parts of my face which are not permanently covered in hair. Orlando Gibbons was posthumously seeing that I was in a calm frame of mind on Radio Three. Over Florida Orange, a boiled egg and strong white coffee I scanned the other financial pages, to see if they were on to anything. The *Express*, noting the small increase in the retail trade figures, was leading on 'Yes, it's boom, boom, Britain.' There was nothing *about* Terby in any of them, although the City Editor of the *Telegraph* had an oblique reference to his type of asset stripping. But screaming out loud and clear from the pages of another paper was something I could hardly credit. An article *by* Terby on the need to curb the growth of City operators who specialize in building up holdings in companies through the use of nominee names. Could you beat it? The guy who had made the nominee name racket into an art form, amassing shareholdings in companies on the cheap, then letting it be known that he, Derek Terby, was the mystery buyer, at which point he either sold as everybody else got on the bandwagon, or bought control, sacked half the workforce, broke up the assets, revalued the factory sites and sold them to property companies at a fat profit. Can you beat that?

So Terby was now trying to remove the ground beneath the feet of all his imitators. Talk about trying to acquire respectability. There would certainly be no need for me to dump a 'corruption in the City' book on my publishing friends now. Dynamic Derek would do it for me, in his spare time lounging around in the respectable clubs Lord Brachan would no doubt be putting him up for. Apart from anything else, the mere fact that he'd put his name to this piece (which would have been written by one of his highly paid assistants from LSE, the more revolutionary their record the better) was good circumstantial evidence of the way his respectability trip was going. It also meant that he knew which way the Tories were moving in their frantic attempts to persuade the electorate that they were more socialist than the

Labour Party – which to be honest, wasn't difficult at the time.

It was 9.30 a.m., and I had arranged my first appointment with a broker at ten. The Terby article would be a big talking point in the City: I only hoped everybody wasn't going to put two and two together immediately.

I dived down the stairs and into the Mini, and drove via the back of the Angel and Goswell Road to the London Wall underground car park. I then went to the old Dickensian coffee house near Birches, for my first crucial meeting.

Stephen Hill-Smythe was your typically suave junior partner in a stockbroking firm, with a town house in Chelsea and a pretty good weekend set-up in Suffolk, I gathered. We'd first met at some party, and he did pretty nicely out of passing his circulars on to the *Jet* when his favoured clients had already been looked after. Occasionally he invited me to lunch in the partners' elegant dining room, and fished for Whitehall gossip about the economic outlook. Sometimes he knew that I knew some embargoed bit of news which would affect the gilt market, and he was not beyond leaving the dining room half-way through on some vague pretext, so that he could deal immediately. If ever a guy owed me a discretionary favour, it was Stephen Hill-Smythe, aged thirty-five, married with two daughters, hours 9.45 to 4.30 (3.30 on Fridays), annual earnings £30,000.

He was already there in the basement coffee parlour, and rose to greet me.

'Tarquin. How nice to see you. I'm mystified. What makes you want to see me so bright and early? I thought you fellows started work at midday. Have you got a good tip or something?'

'Well no, not really. It's just that you said if I ever wanted to do any business. . .'

'Oh; great; fine. Yes; delighted of course. But I thought you told me you didn't believe in all this share-buying nonsense?'

I'd been prepared for this, and one or two other eventualities.

'Yes; well; you know. I've always told you I'm not interested in shares. I'm not really employed for that. Tring basically uses me as a sort of resident adviser, to make sure his attacks on economists are economically literate.'

'Well, what can I do for you?'

'It's not for me actually, it's for my aunt. She's got a portfolio stuffed with all the wrong fixed interest stocks, and at the current rate of inflation the real value of her money will be approaching zero in ten years' time. I wondered whether you could take on her portfolio.'

'Delighted Tarquin. Got any papers with you?'

'No, I'll be seeing her at the weekend and I'll put them in the post to you.'

'Fine. Was that all?'

'Well, almost. But there's just one other aspect to this. I'd quite like to get her into one or two things fairly quickly, so that I can at least tell her I've done *something* when I see her. The truth is I've been promising to do this for her for ages, and meanwhile the market's been recovering and we've missed some good buys.'

'What are you thinking of in particular?'

'Well, what do you think of the oil companies?'

'They're a bit dear at the moment.'

'Things like GEC and Marks and Sparks?'

'Maybe. I'll think it over. Anything else?'

'What about Terby's outfit?'

Hill-Smythe returned his coffee cup to the table with a thump. 'Tarquin, I'm an unabashed bull of Terby's outfit. Oh, I know; I've heard all the criticisms. But that man's a genius and before long he'll have the entire City sewn up. I've got all my major clients in Terby Holdings.' And, as if that wasn't music enough to my ears, he added: 'What's more, Tarquin, I happen to know there's a big seller of Terby Holdings in the market at the moment. Must be off his head. Personally, I reckon it's a perfect share for your aunt. I think we should buy this morning.'

There was a short pause, while I indulged in a hesitation-cum-thinking act. From the point of view of not arousing suspicions, Hill-Smythe had played straight into my hands. They say the art of diplomacy is to get the other guy to make your suggestion.

What could be better than this?

'I, er, haven't been quite sure about Terby myself, Stephen, but on reflection I'm sure you're absolutely right. Look, for God's sake, let's give the old lady some compensation for all those terrible years of War Loan and the like. She's got a hundred thousand. Why don't we put half of it into Terby Holdings?'

Hill-Smythe's eyes lit up. To brokers who handle insurance company and pension fund business, someone with fifty thousand to play with counts as a small investor. But he'd obviously assumed he was merely doing me a good turn, and that perhaps I'd been thinking in terms of five thousand. Fifty, and fifty to go, would give him not a bad piece of commission for one cup of coffee – certainly in four figures.

At this stage Hill-Smythe felt impelled to go through the motions of some half hearted dutiful advice, which I sensed he wished me to ignore as soon as he had stopped speaking: 'Of course, I don't need to tell you Tarquin that some brokers don't think Terby's shares are for widows and orphans...'

'No, and in theory the money would be spread about more evenly...'

'In theory.'

'But...'

'But...'

'So...'

'So, I think we know each other well enough to dispense with formalities. If you like I'll buy those shares for you this morning, and you'll be able to inform her at the weekend that things are under way. Make sure you drop her documents in the post to me soon though. By the way,' he got out a little black notebook, 'where shall I send the contract note to?'

'Mrs Phillips, 133a Godfrey Street, sw3.'

'Fine, okay, I'll do that soon as I get back to the office. Nice to see you Tarquin.'

He departed. The whole thing had gone extremely smoothly, and taken about seven minutes. My next appointment, also in the coffee house, was at ten thirty, so I just sat where I was, reflecting once again on my plans. Of course, the story about my aunt's portfolio was totally fictitious – my aunt hadn't got a bean – but in the world in which Stephen Hill-Smythe, (and now I, Tarquin) moved, it was more likely than not that every other person you met had an aunt with a spare hundred thousand.

Her name *was* Mrs Phillips, however, and I knew she would sign anything, having total trust [sic] in me. But she lived in the country and I wanted all the post to be within easy reach, that's why I gave the Godfrey Street address – a house belonging to an old friend. You will gather that my basic aim in all this was simplicity; but in spite of what I said earlier about people getting away with murder in the City, I thought it advisable – just in case the Takeover Panel or the Stock Exchange Council got wind of anything – at least to keep my name out of it.

As a working assumption, I was taking a purely arbitrary figure of twenty per cent as the premium which Lord Brachan's outfit would put on Terby Holdings in order to secure a successful bid.

This seemed reasonable on the basis of a study I made of previous bids where all that rubbish about 'two and two making five' was dredged up. The shares were £2, and I was therefore assuming they'd hit £2.40 – not over-ambitious – by comparison with some of the bid price movements in the 1960s. A twenty per cent increase in £50, 000 worth of shares would be £10,000, and I would sell them within the account period. Multiply that by ten – remember, I had nine more deals to make with nine more Hill-Smythe figures in the next two days – and I would make £100,000. A lot of little deals, spread around the market. Although the ten batches of £50,000 added up to £½ million, I hoped that the way I was operating they would dribble sporadically through the market and not suggest any dramatic surge of interest in the stock – such as would have occurred if the £500,000 was shoved in all at once. Ideally one would have spread this operation out over a week or so, so as to run even less risk of disrupting the market. But I couldn't be certain that the story wouldn't break in some other way. The great thing was that these were the days of the bull market, with heavy trading and a big turnover in many stocks. I had a good chance of not arousing any suspicions, particularly now that Stephen Hill-Smythe had told me there was a big seller of Terby in the market.

Most of my conversations with other brokers during the course of that Wednesday and Thursday went roughly in accordance with this plan. The only one who was dead against my putting anything into Terby Holdings was John Crampton – the character who'd made that elliptical remark I mentioned earlier about rendering unto Terby the things that were Terby's, and seeking the Messiah elsewhere. I should have remembered. This time Crampton, a senior partner in Hopkirk and Grote, one of the biggest brokers in the City, gave me a long lecture about how absurd it was for the market to value Terby Holdings at something like thirty-three times its annual profits – over double the formula which applied for most other shares then. 'This is a boom year Tarquin,' he said, 'just you wait until Terby's profits drop, and you will find the wretched shares are valued at *half* the yardstick used for the rest of the market.'

'Yes. Maybe. Well, I, er . . .'

'Moreover my dear boy if you take the trouble to look at Terby's article in the paper this morning you'll find him sanctimoniously criticising all the sharp practices he used to indulge in himself.'

'Meaning?'

'Meaning Terby knows the game's up and it's politically embarrassing for the Tories to hear his name bandied about as the apotheosis of capitalism.'

'So?'

'So,' Crampton leaned a little closer. 'So in my view the logical thing is for him to change his image and become more of a banker. What it boils down to is that his current profits are the result of sheer spivvery, and the premium on his shares reflects the public's greed in wanting to get in on the act. No more and no less.'

'I see,' I said. So Crampton apparently knew nothing about the Amalgamated Industrial deal – unless he was having me on.

'Tarquin, one last thing. I'll let you into a little secret. Not only would I not advise your aunt to buy Terby Holdings, I'd strongly urge you, if you had any, to sell them. We at Hopkirks are selling aggressively on behalf of our clients now.'

I thanked Crampton for his advice. So his firm was the seller Stephen Hill-Smythe had been referring to. It was good to know that my own buying of Terby Holdings was going on in the face of this. With the weight of Hopkirk and Grote around, there would be no question of my own little deals disturbing the share price. But while acting on Crampton's advice and not asking him to buy any of the shares, I did not want the neatness of my ten times £10,000 profit plan to be wrecked. So I did a larger double deal with the last of my brokers, a manifest wide boy called Stan Stockton. Stan had a pretty good relationship with the rest of the lads on the *Jet*, and was usually in on their various share rides. As he was the last of my contacts during those two days, and the rest of my business had gone through, I didn't care if he drew the obvious conclusion that I was betting on something, and bought a few Terby Holdings himself.

As you may imagine, it was a pretty busy time for me in those coffee bars and pubs. To make sure one broker didn't see me with another, I covered a wide range of places during the eleven to three period, including Birches, the Throgmorton Bar, Scotch Corner, the Olde Butlers Head and Jamaica Inn (by the George and Vulture, Dickens' old haunt, where the Dickens descendants were still meeting from time to time to please the tourists).

As Augustus Tring was always saying, 'vun ounce of eenformation ees verth a ton of theory.' (Well, he *used* to say *vun*, anyway.) John Crampton and the backroom boys at Hopkirk and Grote had the shadiness and shakiness of Terby's empire all worked out, but they didn't know what Mr Southfields and I knew. The next stage of my plan would be to mention the Terby/Amalgamated story at Tring's morning conference on the Thursday, so that I could be asked to write it up for the paper.

I did manage to bring myself to drop in on Tring's conference on the Wednesday, as my deals were just getting underway.

Tring himself – fresh from his previous day's success at the Races – was in a pretty ebullient and magnanimous state. A bit too much so, I thought. He didn't seem at all like the news-hungry editor we were used to.

'Tarquin,' he said when it was my turn. 'I'm fed up with giving all these share tips to spivs and the likes of you and me. I want to do something for the small fellow; to try and protect the man in Penge who hasn't got two pennies to rub together, and who never reads The Page normally.' As usual Tring pronounced the phrase 'The Page' in a tone of hushed reverence.

I gave the weak smile which always appears on one's face in response to ideas which are totally ludicrous. It was obviously some absurd suggestion he'd picked up from one of his drinking friends.

Tring beamed and continued. 'I'm sure lots of people have piles of pennies lying around the house in piggy banks, earning no interest . . .'

I could see that this would be the immutable opening line. I just sat there, taking it in, knowing that all I had to do was reproduce the stuff with some sort of adherence to the rules of grammar. It seemed a long way away from the great coup I was so busy organising. The little man in Penge would just have to stay there for a few days. As for little Tring, he stood up, drew himself up to his full five feet four inches, and said: 'I am relying on you, Tarquin.'

16

'So things are going quite well?'

'Yes, touch wood.'

The scene has shifted westwards. It is late evening, and a party of three film-goers is sitting in a favourite corner of old Soho. The first speaker is a tall, elegantly seedy gentleman with a distinguished mop of grey hair. The second is yours truly. Between them sits a flaxen-haired girl of medium height in her early twenties, her laughing blue eyes and gently freckled complexion giving the impression that it is good to lead a life of studied innocence – giving, indeed, the added impression that innocence has been studied long enough. Mr Southfields' daughter Judith – my ex – and, so it seems, my present girl friend. Mrs Cordoba, illicit friend till yester-night, thou seemest light years away.

They'd rung up out of the blue to suggest taking in the new Bunuel. Certainly, said I, not having seen it for several weeks. It was one of those Bunuels which give you a good appetite, which in our case was fed with grilled sardines and Mignon de Veau Savoyard, accompanied by a white bordeaux and a 1962 Chambolle Musigny (I see it not and yet I taste it still). A nice spread, for which I thought the *Jet* office ought to pay – were not the eminent Southfields invaluable contacts for the scoop I was about to bestow on Augustus Tring?

After my complacent account of proceedings to date, it suddenly occurred to me that old man Southfields might not actually approve. But I need not have worried.

'Tarquin, I admire your initiative. I spent far too much of my life in that stockbroker's office. I only wish I'd opted out by doing something really smart like this ages ago. One's principles evaporate with the years, and I don't mind admitting I've been doing a bit of buying of Terby's shares myself since we last talked.'

'Well that's great then. Let's have some port.'

'I can't help getting a certain amount of pleasure out of it all, particularly since . . .'

'Since?'

'Since I've been fired.'

'What? What? Why? How? Again?'

'Relax, it's not quite as bad as that. I've been fired by Terby, but in fact I didn't really work for him – I work for a firm of contract hire chauffeurs. It appears that Terby used to like driving himself, then tried the chauffeuring kick, but has decided it's a waste of manpower to have someone like me hanging around all day waiting for him. I'll get some other tycoon tomorrow.'

'This is efficiency gone mad when tycoons fire their chauffeurs,' I said.

I stole a look down Judith's forefront; then another. The idea that we two were in some way getting intertwined again was hardly anathema.

'Terby was in a rare old state of excitement last night, after he emerged from Blizzards. It was about 11 p.m.; there were certainly no sleepy members of the press like yourself patrolling the building; he came out beaming with the Amalgamated Industrial fellow, Henry Allan – who was also looking like the cat who'd caught the cream. I swear they were almost arm in arm.'

'This is fantastic. It all seems to be fitting into place, doesn't it?'

'The only thing being that, having been given the boot so abruptly this morning, my own usefulness as a source of information is finished.'

'Maybe that's just as well. Incidentally, I forgot to tell you. I've got to do the rest of my buying tomorrow morning, but so far the price has been on our side. I had a glance at Jim Parsons' market report. He says the price went up 3p on "Persistent small buying" – i.e. me and, apparently, you – but later fell back. He summed it up as "an active two way market".'

'Excellent. And you're going to give the story to Tring tomorrow morning?'

That glass of port was indeed pleasant. I then took them both in the Mini to Victoria Station. Judith's farewell kiss was not exactly off-putting. As I drove back to Canonbury I reflected that, on the principle that, being a normal human being and not a James Bond, I had to confide my misdeeds to *someone*, it was all best kept in what looked like being the family.

17

The next day was a Thursday, my thirtieth birthday. Jesus. Thirty and not hitched: in the eyes of the world I must be totally immature or a manifest poove or both.

The gardens on our side of the square face south east, as did my bedroom. The sun was shining in, and I climbed into a pair of shorts, thinking to take orange juice and coffee down to the garden, which was cultivated beautifully by my neighbours below. The roses were still with us; and I was watching the hollyhock, with an eye on the next time the height of the species came up in the correspondence columns of *The Times*.

I was half-way down the stairs when there was a knock at the door. Tentatively – I wasn't too hot on paying bills at this stage of my life – I opened it. Immediately I was bowled over by a chorus of HAPPY BIRTHDAY TO YOU, sung by the Rogan children ensemble, and an invitation to breakfast.

'Mummy says you're fifty.'

'No, thirty.'

'Daddy says you ought to get married before you're set in your ways.'

'Oh.'

'Never mind Mr Tarquin, sappy birthday,' said the youngest, aged about two and a half.

It seems to me that you have to judge a marriage not by the number of times the participants are throwing knives and forks at each other, but by the number of times they don't. Concern about being 'set in your ways' was a standard joke among my married contemporaries with regard to me, and they were always arranging catastrophic meetings. The Rogans didn't exactly throw in a spare bird to go with my thirtieth birthday breakfast party (I wouldn't have objected in that heat) but I was struck again by the relatively low level of disenchantment around the place, and I certainly liked the kids. On the wall across the rather crowded table the spectre of Judith Southfields' ghost loomed large.

I thanked them dearly for my presents – which included everything from wine to razor blades – and rang Interflora as soon as I got into the office to return the compliment to Mrs Rogan. I even thought of inviting the Rogans out to dinner, but at this stage it was an open question whether I'd be spending the evening with Judith, my parents, or some of the lads. There was even, perish the thought, the possibility that Mrs Cordoba would be in touch again.

Conference that morning was not until midday, because it was Augustus Tring's day for keeping fit – after being chauffeur-driven to the gymnasium, of course. This gave me plenty of time to execute the remainder of my buying orders for Terby Holdings. By 11.45 I was in the office, ready for the crucial conference at which I would reveal my knowledge of the Amalgamated bid for Terby. What was more, the tapes were showing Terby Holdings unchanged at £2. Crampton must still be selling. But I had met no more Cramptons in my round of contacts. It just shows you how the City at that time was in thrall to this feverish belief in Terby's magical powers. 'If only they had known the little twit at school,' I kept thinking.

A quick whiff of the perfumes of Arabia gave us advance warning that Tring had swept in. 'Morning boys. Beautiful day. What a pity I've got to spend the lunch hour closeted with the Chancellor in some stuffy restaurant.'

Buzzer, red light, conference. 'Now then, what have we got today?'

The deputy financial editor was a nice but extremely harassed guy who almost wore his mill-board round his long neck; he was a full foot taller than Tring, but that didn't seem to give him an added presence. He filled us in on the schedule of known news for the day: some major company results, and a press briefing on the Department of Trade's latest thoughts on merger policy, if any.

Jim Parsons dropped in the names of a few spiv companies that he regarded as 'good buys'.

Jack Spick said he thought there was a healthy revival in company profits, which might make a think piece for Monday. At this stage the *Jet* was justifying its nauseatingly tabloid approach to news by advertising itself as the paper 'for busy thinkers'. Spick and I had changed the slogan to 'for people who are too busy to think'. Tring liked the phrase 'think piece', so in lieu of anything else we were always able to threaten him with one.

Tring looked at me.

'Well, we've got the trade figures,' I said keeping my scoop back a second for the magic moment when it would have maximum impact.

'What's the time? They out yet?'

I looked up at his clock. Five to twelve (in those days the overseas trade figures were announced at midday). 'Not quite.'

Tring looked out of the window for a few seconds, his gaze fixed intently on some workmen who were demolishing the building next door. 'The *Jet* building will be next,' Spick muttered.

'Fred,' Tring said to the deputy financial editor in passing, 'remind me to tell you about our new offices later.'

'Now listen,' he said to me, 'any more thoughts on my idea of a piece for the man in Penge?'

'Well, yes, I'm working at it. But quite honestly . . .'

'Well I had an idea at the gymnasium this morning. How about "your best investment is your house".'

Tring was about to ramble on, waxing lyrically on solving the problems of people he was totally out of touch with. I interrupted. 'There is one other thing.'

'Oh yes, what's that?' Tring's face had the familiar glazed look of somebody whose mind was by now on at least three other things.

'I, er . . .' I paused for breath, trying to get the timing right. 'I, er . . .'

'Oh there's one other company result today,' said somebody. 'Do you mind if I rush off, I've got a 12.15 appointment,' said another. There was a babel of voices. I tried shouting but no one was interested. I grabbed the deputy financial editor's arm, as the others were trooping out. 'Do you realise what I've got,' I yelled. 'Blue eyes,' he said quick as a flash. 'I . . . I . . .' By now the huge door of Tring's sanctuary was closed, and I was left in the large oak-panelled room with Tring, the deputy and Tring's secretary.

Ever have that feeling that you're hanging around and nobody's taking a blind bit of notice? I might have been a fly on the wall for all those guys cared. I hung on gamely, trying to edge in on their conversation – about the plans for a new, bigger City office in a Barbican block (Spick permitting, I thought). Gradually I insinuated myself as a third voice in their dialogue.

'Look, the thing is, I'VE GOT A SCOOP.'

'Great,' said the deputy, continuing the air of levity into which the discussion about new offices had developed. 'Why don't you go and water it?'

'Look, this is serious.'

'Hang on a minute,' said Tring. 'What is it.'

I steadied myself, and with the maximum of aplomb declaimed: 'Amalgamated Industrial is going to bid for Terby Holdings.'

The deputy financial editor, who when levity wasn't too much to the fore had some respect for me, looked interested. Tring said: 'Oh not that hoary old chestnut, Tarquin. Tell us another.'

'But . . . but you asked me to keep an eye on Terby and you yourself said something was going on. I know. I'm absolutely sure.'

'No, dear boy, when I said Terby was up to something, I mean I think he's got some European deal up his sleeve. Now if you'd told me this one six months ago I might have believed you. As a matter of fact I believe that one of Terby's henchmen – Cordoba

– was trying to fix something through one of the merchant banks. But it all fell through. Look, no respectable company would touch that spiv Terby with a barge pole.'

Coming from a City editor who had more or less discovered Terby, tipped his shares ad nauseam and built him up into a sort of God figure for the Saturday reader, I thought that was pretty good.

'Look I'm absolutely sure.'

Tring still looked sceptical. 'Where did you get it from. Some lousy broker who's trying to unload Terby shares at what must undoubtedly be their peak?'

I shook my head. 'No, much better than that.'

'Got any photostats, any tangible proof? It would be a terrible story to get wrong.'

That's what I liked about Tring: his double standards. You have to have the cheek of the devil to get away with being a popular Financial editor. Many a time on a slow news day I'd seen him manufacture a story out of a rumour he'd concocted himself. Anybody who cared to look through the *Jet* cuttings of the previous few years would find a record of almost absolute inconsistency, with Tring – as the post-lunch mood or the weather took him – castigating the managements of companies whose shares he'd been recommending a few months earlier. It's in the nature of a daily paper that everything – especially consistency – is sacrificed to the needs of a story that looks good for twenty-four hours. I recall the time he made an engineering company that was about to go bust into his 'share for next year', on the basis of a few lies from the chairman over lunch, thereby ensuring that the small investors who followed him were propping the share price up while those who knew the real situation were able to get out at a high price. I'm not suggesting he deliberately did this: just *one*, that he was utterly conned by the chairman and *two*, that the way his mind worked he could conveniently absolve himself from any blame. Oh yes. Tring would be only too eager to put the knife into anybody if it would shrink the yawning blank space in his page make-up at 6 p.m.

76

And here he was, demanding proof, on the only day when it really mattered to me that he should actually print one of my stories in his wretched column.

Before sloping off for a much-needed drink with Spick, I stole a quick look at the tapes. Holy Godfathers. The trade figures were out; the initial reaction of the market was that they were bloody awful. The whole index was down, and Terby Holdings had fallen 5p with everything else, to £1.95. So far my coup was going backwards.

Calm yourself, Tarquin, I said to myself. This is but a flurry of the moment. It's Thursday, and the Stock Exchange account has a week and a bit to run. There is plenty of time for the story to get out, and if necessary – given Tring's reluctance to accept one of the few scoops I've ever proferred – we'll have to let it slip to somebody on another paper. Any attempt to check the story out is bound to provoke either a bogus denial or a speedy announcement. Let us take consolation from the fact that if any of those idle brokers have been too slow in carrying out our buying orders this morning, they will actually be picking Terby's shares up somewhat cheaper than we had expected. Meanwhile, after our drink, we must do some administration – i.e. nip across to 133a Godfrey Street and see if any of yesterday's brokers' contract notes have arrived. They are very quick off the mark with these.

18

My friends in 133a Godfrey Street were away for a few weeks,
but when I said I needed to borrow a pad while mine was being
redecorated – white lie – they'd said fine, a caretaker would be
useful, and left the key under the formidable potted plant outside.

I charged in, hoping to be tripped up by the heap of brokers'
contract notes addressed to Mrs Phillips – my dear unsuspecting
aunt, whose signature I would forge on all necessary occasions.
There wasn't one. My plan awry already? No, I hadn't reckoned
with the Daily, who could be heard choking over the occupants'
gin bottle in the dining room on the right. I explained my
presence, and was told I was expected. She even offered me a
gin and tonic – just wait until I tell the Steadmans *that*, I thought.

In spite of the fact that Chelsea has been almost entirely
wrecked by becoming one gigantic boutique, I reflected that there
was still something to be said for those early Victorian side streets,
each old artisan's cottage tarted up a different colour.

I was trying to get a word in edgeways as the Daily gave me
a detailed account of the life and times of what she kept calling
her 'relationship with my boy friend'. She was aged fifty-five
if she was a day. There's hope for us all yet, I thought, but where
the hell had she put the contract notes addressed to Mrs Phillips?

I nodded vigorously in what I took to be the right places, in
the hope that she would eventually wear herself down with some
laborious account of how her boy friend refused to pay for the
deckchairs on Bournemouth beach.

Eventually she paused for breath. 'They told me you was
comin'. Yer room's upstairs.'

'Fine. Er, there's just one thing. Has there been any mail?'

She gave me what she no doubt described later to her boy friend as 'a queer look', and said: 'What name?'

'Phillips.'

'Phillips? Mrs Phillips?' (The *Mrs* pronounced with all the emphasis Lady Bracknell applies to handbags.)

'Yes, that's right.'

I could see fifty years' Sunday morning training with the *News of the World* come to the fore as she proceeded to look me up and down. She then pursed her lips, got up very deliberately, and left the room, returning a few minutes later with my bundle of mail. Looking me disconcertingly straight in the face, she said: 'I suppose it's all right to give these to you.'

'You see, they're for my aunt,' I said without conviction. 'Well, many thanks, I must be off.'

I suppose you could say that 133a Godfrey Street was a genuine accommodation address, since I had virtually had to take up residence there to organise the mail. I deserted my female companion at once, and made for the Antelope off Sloane Square where I sat on a bench outside with a pint, opened the mail, and took stock of the situation.

Not bad. The plan for ten separate purchases of Terby shares had been revised when Crampton gave me his advice, so that I had eight deals going through individual brokers and one double one via Stan Stockton. In addition to the Stockton deal, I'd managed to get five of the other purchases arranged the previous day through Stephen Hill-Smythe and others. And the last three of the ten had been fixed that morning, before my abortive attempt to interest Tring in the story itself. Well, in those magnificent days before all stockbrokers were computerised and our wonderful postal services had not quite collapsed, no less than five contract notes had already arrived in the post confirming the previous day's transactions. This meant that I was already the proud owner – shall I say that again – of £250,000 worth of shares in a company run by Derek Terby, the man I loved to hate. It would be a matter of days before contract notes arrived confirming my ownership of another £250,000 of Terby shares.

Downing my pint helped to ease my concern about the fact that, however sound the basis of my operations, the wretched shares had actually been showing a loss after the trade figures announcement.

Well, the pint helped. But I suddenly thought that, hell, it was my birthday and while there was a pretty crowded programme in prospect for the evening, I made a sorry sight boozing away there in a pub by myself at lunchtime. It was now 1.30 p.m. Unlikely that Spick would be in the office, but I rang him on the off-chance and he was. He was mid-way through some piece for *Socialist Worker* on 'How the Other Half Live', and was only too willing to take a break at that point for lunch – we, rather he, chose that well-known workers' café, L'Escargot Bienvenu in Greek Street.

In view of the importance of Mrs Cordoba and Judith South-fields to my story, you may have forgotten that bit earlier on, when I mentioned how Jack Spick had taken over where I left off with Lindy Fanshawe. It's impossible to lunch in Soho on a steaming hot summer's day without having the subject of sex in the forefront of one's mind, for reasons I take it I don't need to go into. So it was the most natural thing in the world for us to get round to everybody's favourite topic pretty fast, and Jack gave me a rundown of his Fanshawe affair. Their weekend in Paris had been a great success – as far as Spick's mother was concerned that was with me, remember? Since then the two had been clinging to each other, Spick taking her off to all those terrible revolutionary meetings of his in Holloway and Hackney.

Spick told me a few sexual gems with mild pride but in a somewhat matter-of-fact way. Then his face shone with enthusiasm as he reached the climax of his tale. 'She's really quite a strong left winger, you know.'

Strong left winger my foot, I thought. She'd string along with any bedtime philosophy, that girl, but never mind. I was then informed that Spick's mother was so pleased that Spick and I were due to go on another weekend trip somewhere else. One of these days I'd tell her we slept in a double bed.

Now it was my turn. Although Spick may have been up the creek on national politics he was no chicken in the machinations at a local level, including that well-known bastion of Trotskyism, the *Jet* City Office.

I didn't tell him of the dealings Mr Southfields and I were up to, but I reminded him of our original talk about Terby, and told him about my scoop, and how I had singularly failed to convince Tring that morning.

'Well, you'd better keep it for Monday, hadn't you?' said the wise old revolutionary, his hands en route towards the Chateaubriand.

Yes, he was right. You could get almost anything into the Monday column, provided you stayed sober enough on Friday to write it – or at least to advise Tring on how to write it. But more of that in a minute.

We took a cab back to the office. The general view continued to be that the trade figures were fairly disastrous. The stock market was still down – with Terby Holdings remaining at the morning's £1.95 – and the pound was slipping back on the foreign exchange market. Enough to make Tring as gloomy as hell on a wet afternoon, but it happened to be blazing hot sunshine outside. We got back at three thirty, and Tring rolled in from the Savoy at about four – late for his afternoon appointment, which was a visit from a Tory MP who was beginning to regret his association with some punk company considered to be going bust. This guy thought Tring was the fount of wisdom, but on this occasion the only thing the fount poured out was afternoon tea. Then it was my turn.

'What do you make of these trade figures, Tarquin?' said Tring.

'Pretty disastrous,' said I, remembering the party line a couple of months back, when Tring had chosen to detect a bad trend behind what everybody else thought were encouraging figures.

Tring stretched back, patted his ample stomach, pulled at his elegant red braces, and puffed his cigar, looking all the while out of the window at the sunny scene below.

'Oh I don't know. I think people want to read something cheerful at this time of year. You know...I think the gloom can be overdone.'

He looked at his secretary for reassurance. She nodded her head discreetly, her suntan looking rather inviting. We all fancied his secretary.

'You see, this is not a bad old country. I can't believe things are as disastrous as all that.'

Sensing the way the wind was blowing, and urgently needing to curry favour for the events of the morrow, I began to nod assent, mumbling phrases like 'I see what you mean' and other such inanities. On Friday Tring would be searching for ideas for the Monday column, and as Spick had pointed out, that would be the best time to strike. When it came to getting your ideas accepted in that office, however, everything depended not so much on Tring's general mood, as on his mood vis-à-vis you in particular at the time.

So I toadied away, and Tring could see that the ritual was going well; that the necessary reassurance was forthcoming. Being the egocentric nutcases we are, journalists need encouragement at every step. On he plodded.

'Susanna, get me my dictionary of quotations and that book on how to lie with statistics, will you?'

The white flag was up, we were under starter's orders, we were off. Tring took up the silver ball-point pen with which he scrawled the highest-paid sentences in Fleet Street, and set off down the track, one sentence per page, every alternate page torn up, then the magnificent product passed to Susanna, with me acting as a highly paid messenger boy, whose advice on the subject in hand was often asked but seldom heeded.

'There are lies, damned lies and statistics,' he wrote with relish. 'Yesterday's trade figures come into the category of...'

I hung on gamely through the vesperal hour, thinking of many things: Judith Southfields, Mrs Cordoba, Mr Southfields, Derek

Terby, and my scoop. I'd got over the initial shock of my second quasi-cuckoldom – Mrs Cordoba and the young boy – and was just beginning to wonder whether that was that. With Judith's voluptuous body on every piece of wallpaper in my mind's eye, I was getting hooked pretty fast. Nevertheless, I had the urge to *see* Mrs Cordoba again – just to say tweet tweet to my little starling and bow out of her life in graceful style, a form of reverse mating ceremony in which we should at least kiss and make up. Characters like Mrs Cordoba are too precious to be lost to our lives for ever, and I could just sense how welcoming Judith's labial fist would be to any suggestion on my part that we should keep in touch with the Starling after the betrothal. Women know too much, usually without being informed.

'What do you think of that?' said Tring, interrupting my thoughts. I hadn't a clue what he was talking about; I said, 'Very good indeed, Augustus. Just what people want to hear.'

'Excellent. Now, when Susanna's finished typing it out, I want you to check every word, every figure, every bit of punctuation. I'm off to Hurlingham for a party. After that, put your thinking cap on and dream up something for Monday's paper. We're desperately short of ideas at the moment.'

19

Birthday night. When you're single you tend to crowd too much into your evening, I used to find. I checked Tring's copy, corrected a wrong quotation, and did a ring round. Was it trying it on a bit to arrange a quick trip to Wimbledon to see my parents, before picking Judith up at Victoria at 9.15, taking in a visit to Mrs Cordoba and a party at the National Institute of Economic and Social Research on the way? Not to say a quick drink with Spick in Birches at seven, just to get the wheels oiled?

Yes, it was crazy. I drove the Mini down to Dean Trench Street, and dropped in first at the Institute. You get most of the economic establishment at those affairs, and I particularly wanted to buttonhole my former Cambridge supervisor, to let him know that in spite of my examination fiasco up there, I'd managed to straighten things out and acquire that respectable degree at LSE later.

Sure enough, the wee fellow was holding court in the library, his glass and his hands at all angles. Having sighted him, I had a brief word with a few government economists on the current state of the stop-go debate; then I insinuated myself into Brandon's court.

'Hello Tarquin. Long time no see. What brings *you* to these parts?'

'Oh I'm just passing by. I've got a job with the *Jet* City Office. Did you hear, by the way, that in spite of that fiasco over my degree . . .'

At this point I learned one of life's great lessons: that once somebody's made an assessment of you, that's it. Nothing can budge their judgement, certainly not the facts.

'Fiasco? What fiasco? You got your degree didn't you? It wasn't a bad one.'

Okay. The point had not got across in the right way, but at least I had rather more respect deposited in my supervisor's mind than I had thought. No doubt we could now resume those enjoyable exchanges we had during what were meant to be tutorials.

Brandon was muttering to himself. 'The *Jet* City Office, eh? You must get some good share tips. Look, I'm bursar to the College now: what do you make of Terby Holdings?'

Holy mother of capitalism. How our left-wing economists adapt themselves to the system. Praise Marx and pass the ticker tape. For the first time in my life I was in a position to instruct my tutor.

I leaned forward. Those National Institute parties are like a bear garden, and I had to deliver my confidential whisper in a roar. 'It's funny you should say that. I have reason to believe they are a very good buy at the moment. But keep in touch. There will be a right time to sell.'

With that I disappeared into the evening, to drive down to Wimbledon for a quick birthday drink with my parents at the Alex, where you could get a decent drop of Youngs real ale. The old man was in great form, planning a trip to his old Durham haunts, unvisited by the family for nigh on thirty-five years.

He asked me if I had any good tips to augment his holiday money, and I offered him Terby Holdings.

He snorted. 'Terby? Not that little weed you used to play cricket with in Cottenham Park?'

'That's him. No less. Shares are going to shoot up. Take it from me.'

The old man laughed heartily for about a minute. 'Look, I've learned my lesson with *your* share tips. What I'm really interested in is the shares you're *not* tipping. I'll tell you what *I'd* like to do with your wretched Terby's shares, and that's that method you told me about once – sell the bloody things short.'

I looked at my watch. 'Thanks for the birthday present,' I

said, 'I must fly.'

'Here today and gone tomorrow,' said my mother.

'Here today and gone today,' muttered the old man.

It was now eight thirty. I drove up through Wandsworth and Battersea to Kensington, and thence via Hyde Park to Mrs Cordoba's place at St Johns Wood. One of the 'step'-daughters opened the door and disappeared upstairs, leaving Starling and me in the first-floor drawing room.

'I just wanted to say goodbye properly,' I said. 'The other night was a bit grisly, but at least we know where we stand.'

'I shall always have a special regard for you, Tarquin. Don't lose touch.'

'Right then. Goodbye.'

'Goodbye, my love.'

I retreated backwards towards the door, en route for Victoria Station to pick up Judith from the train. Mrs Cordoba suddenly flew across the room, out into the hall, and descended on me like a vulture as I began retreating down the stairs. In the old days one would have described what ensued as a quick necking session, but I'm not up with current jargon.

'Careful,' I said, 'I'm meeting my beloved in twenty minutes. My clothes will stink of your scent.'

'Then take them off,' said old thin lips, her vixenish smile getting to work.

I've always been a bit dubious about all that strength of character stuff. Any normal male in my situation that evening would have had to chalk this up as a moment of weakness, even though the balance of the argument was in favour of my dashing off to Victoria to meet Judith's train.

'What here?' I said, groping fast for a passing baluster as I began to slide off balance down the stairs.

Her lips began to curl after the fashion of Snow White's mother in that children's ladybird book illustration.

'You really would Tarquin, wouldn't you? Here we are, just good friends again, and you can't resist it.'

'What do you mean?' I said, coming – literally – to a landing, and dusting myself down. 'Goodnight Mrs Cordoba.'

I stood there for a while. She shrugged her shoulders and stormed upstairs, obviously towards the bedroom. I looked at my watch – nine minutes to go – and waited a while, half-hoping that she'd come flaunting down in her underwear, like in some terrible novel, pretending she was going to the kitchen, but in reality giving the seal of seduction to the next scene.

She did not. The telephone rang, and I slunk out. Such is the way we strong men cope with our moments of weakness.

After all this I was actually early for Judith's train, which conveniently happened to be twenty minutes late. As I stood there waiting, I reflected on the Mrs Cordoba scene, and wondered how she stood on her share dealings with Terby Holdings. I noticed a couple – mother and daughter – come off another platform, staggering under their luggage. They stopped outside the newsstand, obviously waiting for something. A few seconds later a guy who'd been hovering around for some time went up to them and said 'Mrs Nixon?' The older woman replied, 'How very kind,' and handed him a parcel, at which point he ran off. All this happened under my very eyes, and I stood there rooted to the spot. The other two just walked off, and by the time I'd come round to the view that this was how your drug smuggling was done, none of the participants was in sight. Another moment of strength Tarquin: you're really totting them up on this birthday evening.

We had a pleasant dinner at Au Père de Nico, sitting in the open-air part. Judith told me that the old man had managed to acquire more Terby Holdings, during the day, thereby confirming that Mr Southfields and Mr Tarquin were in this thing up to their necks.

Even in the most liberal families there are certain social formalities, and Judith had told her parents she was staying with an aunt. This struck me as fine, because I would have to be on top form to recoup the reputation lost in the Glyndebourne field, and after all the events of recent days did not feel up to much that evening. So I was a bit taken aback when we stopped outside the aunt's – in Prince of Wales Drive, overlooking Battersea Park – and Judith said: 'Well, is that all?'

The seducer seduced?

'Well, not exactly,' I said. 'If you wish to come back to my place, do. But I was thinking of your parents.'

'You were doing nothing of the kind, Tarquin. As usual you were thinking of yourself. Why don't you be honest and admit that after a week of pursuing me you don't actually feel like it tonight?'

'Well, seeing how you . . .'

'Honestly, men are so perverse. When I finally come round to the idea you don't want to.'

She did not mention the Glyndebourne fiasco, pretending that this was the first opportunity. Nevertheless, she was obviously upset.

'Well, I suppose . . .' I looked at my watch. The perfect birthday treat, the seduction of my beloved, was being offered to me on a plate, and I was worried about being fit and fresh for the big story on Terby the following day.

'Oh God, I loathe people who wear watches,' she suddenly shouted, and before I had cottoned on she was storming into the house. Men perverse? Who says so. I just spent half the bloody night thinking what it might have been like.

20

Judith rang the Steadmans' number almost before I was out of bed the following morning.

'Thanks for the evening, Tarquin, I really enjoyed it. Sorry I stormed off like that. How about taking me out to breakfast in the King's Road?'

Well, as I've said, what with the boutiques and the boutiques there's hardly room for anything else in that street nowadays. However, we crawled into the Kenco for coffee and a bite, and she made her retributive offering.

'Darling,' (hello . . .). 'Some friends of Daddy's have offered me their Welsh cottage for the weekend, but the girl I was going with has got mumps. Would you like to come?'

Apart from the obvious implication of this suggestion, the thought of some relaxation in the mountain air – if we had the time – was an added attraction at this difficult stage of my Terby plot. Whether or not Tring would buy my scoop that morning I had no idea, but either way – with only a week of the Stock Exchange account left – I was getting into a nervous state. Whether I succeeded in dropping the story into the *Jet* or on to another paper, I would need a breather before the suspense of the following week.

Furthermore, the office had a duty roster for Sundays and it wasn't my turn. We were on for Wales. Back to reality, however: we were cutting it a bit fine for morning conference.

I made the office by the skin of the Highway Code – 60 mph, even on the Embankment, is going some in London – arriving just in time for my turn in conference.

Tring sat there, smooth and sleek as ever in the mornings, looking every inch the Jermyn Street dummy.

I sat there, a bit breathless from the rush, surveying the great diminutive man and knowing that now I wanted the man who moved the market to move the market for me.

'Hasn't anybody got any bright ideas for Monday,' he was saying. 'How about you Tarquin?'

'Well what about my story about Terby Holdings and Amalgamated Industrial?'

'Oh, for God's sake, not that again, Tarquin. Look I told you yesterday, it's a load of old rubbish.'

He went on round the circle, getting no further in his quest for items.

'Look you guys, we'll have to do better than this. Here you are, the highest paid City office in Fleet Street, and not an idea between you. What am I going to tell the editor next time he questions the numbers in the City office?'

But Tring was in no danger from the editor. Editors of the *Jet* came and forcibly went, but as long as he pulled the financial advertising revenue in, Tring could go on for ever. Or could he? The strain on the great man was tending to show in late afternoon these days – when the continental elegance for which he was renowned was much less to the fore – and Tring badly wanted to move out of the whole scene into his chosen world of City directorships. Come on Tring: help a young friend and colleague before you leave. Buy my scoop please.

Anyway, I made no progress during the morning. At lunchtime I went off to Milletts in Oxford Street to buy a bit of gear for the weekend. I'd never been your outward bound sort, but Judith had warned me that up in Maentwrog you could be wallowing in the mud when the rest of the country was basking in 82 degrees – Costa del London, as the *Evening Standard* was calling it that day. So I stocked up on walking boots, Swedish socks and an anorak, plus a brandy flask for any artificial respiration we might need up there in the Snowdonia clouds.

Back in the office there was a speech from a big American

economic consultant in my in-tray, entitled 'The death of the profit motive?'. I thought it was worth three paragraphs for the Monday paper, and later discovered the great prophet had charged a cool £2,000 for delivering his message to some conference of businessmen at the London Hilton.

Between four and five Tring's office had the red light up, meaning no entry for anybody – a sure sign that he was talking to his own stockbroker. 'A financial editor should never dabble in shares' Tring was fond of pontificating to admiring Ministers who sought his advice. 'Apart from the ethics of the thing, it would warp his judgement.'

Tring was beaming as he conducted the broker to the door, but the bonhomie melted pretty fast as he came back towards the general desk, looked up at the clock, and said, 'For Christ's sake what am I going to write about today?'

His deputy came to the rescue with the news that sterling was still weak and that that could be blown up for the relatively small space he had on Saturday mornings.

'All right. Well let's get that out of the way first. But we must have something for Monday. I'm going away for the weekend and I don't want to have to follow up whatever they shove in the *Sunday Times* Business News. Let's have something before we leave please.' There was a pause, and Tring's gaze settled on Jim Parsons, the writer of the market report. 'Come on Jim. Haven't you got anything out of your spivvy friends this week?'

In an almost inaudible drunken slur, Jim Parsons said: 'It's very difficult, Augustus, but there's not much going on at the moment.' I wondered whether the time was ripe to raise the subject of Amalgamated Industrial again, but the look on Tring's face did not tempt me further.

Tring swore, and disappeared into the inner sanctum to write the piece on sterling in conjunction with his deputy. I rang up Judith to confirm that we'd meet at Godfrey Street at nine, and spent the next half hour in Birches with Jack Spick. We wandered back at about twenty to six, Spick saying he must do his expenses while he had the energy. I sat down, twitching nervously about my Terby operations and wondering who to ring next to while away the time. The deputy financial editor appeared from Tring's office and said the great man wanted a word.

Tring was sitting there looking moderately tense, the elegant jacket removed and his thumbs twitching behind his bright red braces.With little attempt to conceal his general distrust of anything which was to emerge from my lips, he said: 'Now Tarquin, what *was* this story of yours about Terby again?'

The deputy was standing behind him, nodding his head, obviously having tried to convince him that there was only one possible Monday morning lead, and it was mine.

I delineated the Terby/Amalgamated Industrial picture as I understood it, without being so rash as to explain the full details of how I had pieced it together.

'And you're really certain of this?'

'I am absolutely certain that a deal has been arranged under which Amalgamated will bid for Terby in the very near future, and Terby will go on the board as managing director of the whole outfit.'

'They're buying management, aren't they?' said the deputy financial editor in an attempt to jog my case along while Tring sat there silent.

I knew what was going through Tring's mind. His general motto may have been that an ounce of information was worth a ton of theory, but all he employed me for was the theory. I'd never given him a scoop like this before, and he wasn't quite sure whether to believe it. On the other hand he was a great gambler, and knew only too well that people soon forget about forecasts that don't come off. When his forecasts were right, however, he certainly made sure he reminded his readers.

'Well I don't know,' said Tring. 'Sometimes I wonder what I'm paying you characters for.'

'It's a good story Augustus,' muttered the deputy financial editor, hopping nervously from one foot to the other.

Tring turned to his secretary. 'Susanna, what time am I meant to be at that function?'

'You asked Larry to pick you up at half past six. It's ten to six now.'

Tring looked out of the window for inspiration, rolled up his sleeves and reached for the magic silver biro.

He stared ahead at the portrait of a younger himself on the wall, and addressed it as in a trance – his wont when preparing the big intro, as we in journalism used to call the opening line.

'The whisper of rumour becomes a roar,' he intoned, looking at his deputy, his secretary and myself for a reaction, and then scrawling the great sentence diagonally on a large sheet of blank paper.

'Great, Augustus,' said the deputy.

I myself murmured a sound reminiscent of the Goon show but intended to show strong approval. The secretary had a slight frown on her face. Tring looked out of the window again, picked up the piece of paper, and screwed it up in his strong right hand.

'Fetch me my quotations book, Susanna,' he said, and the secretary staggered over under the weight of the Oxford tome. Tring fumbled around with it for a while, then resumed the incantations.

'Ye who listen with credulity to the whispers of fancy . . .' he essayed, looking up for audience reaction.

'No,' said the deputy. 'Might puzzle the reader in Penge.'

The secretary shook her head in vague disapproval. Tring tore up the second bit of paper.

After a pause we experienced a third act of creation. 'The multitude of whispers gathers into a crescendo . . .'

He tore this up without looking at any of us. The biro broke as soon as it was lowered on to the next piece of paper. 'Blast,' he said, and reached for another. The clock ticked tactlessly on to two minutes past six. He was beginning to flap: the sort of occasion – by no means rare – when the polish would come off his experienced English accent.

'Oh, all right zen,' he moaned, and was off. 'The weesper of rumours becomes a [guttural] roar . . . paragraph . . . my spies tell me zat beneath that slumbering face of ailing giant Amalgamated

Industrial, somesing ees astir . . . paragraph . . . and who should be doing ze stirring? None ozair zan our old friend and viz kid, dynamic Derek Ter . . .' I suppose I exaggerate, but that is the way pub story repetition over the years has convinced me he talked on that occasion. At all events, even though Tring was writing the story I wanted, I could bear it no longer. Oh how painful it was to witness yet another stage in the canonisation of Terby. Terby, Terby, Terby. My living witness to the durability of passing childhood hatreds.

I furnished Tring with the relevant details on which the speculative story could be built up, and then retired to the lavatory for a pee. Such action was a good consumer of time in the *Jet* financial office at this period, because the only lavatory available to non-Trings was several floors away and the lift didn't work.

I'll say this for Tring. Given the assistance he surrounded himself with, once he got going he could churn the stuff out mighty fast.

When I got back he'd almost finished. The secretary was busy typing it out so that he could pore over it with me, and he left the final checking to yours truly, while he went off on the night's binge. I was in a high old state of excitement as I left the office and drove off to Godfrey Street, to meet Judith.

As we drove up the M1 in the Mini, Judith began to quiz me on the state of financial play, assuring me that she was certain by this time that old man Southfields had bought enough Terby shares to retire on.

'That's convenient, because he's more or less retired already, hasn't he?'

'Oh, don't be mean.'

'I'm not being mean.'

There followed one of those sulky silences which we grown-ups are so practised in. This made the journey past the Newport Pagnell service place all the more nervewracking – scene of at least three of my overheating breakdowns in cars, Newport Pagnell has become a second home over the years. I'm always terrified the car is going to break down fifteen miles either side of the place. That, plus a recurrence of nerves about our Terby operations during our Stony Stratford silence must have produced some pretty desperate vibrations; with good timing Judith signalled that the row was over by making a reference to the weather.

I resumed my explanation. 'Thanks to the unwitting good offices of my aunt, I myself am now the owner of £500,000 worth of stock in Terby Holdings.'

'How much do you stand to make out of that?'

'Well if the bid is twenty per cent above the price I paid, I'll automatically be the owner of £600,000 worth of stock. There'll be brokers' commission and so on, but I'll get the best part of £100,000.'

'What about capital gains tax Tarquin?'

'The tax boys won't be able to catch me in the obscure corner of the Dordogne I've got my eyes on.'

'Oh Tarquin, what romantic nonsense.'

Oh Jesus, I thought. What had I said? The whole purpose of my plot laid bare – to the very person with whom there appeared to be enough romantic nonsense in train already. Did this mean . . . did this mean she saw a genuine threat to one load of romantic nonsense from the other?

'A joke darling. A joke,' I said lightly.

The look my burgeoning partner threw at me made your average doubting Thomas the epitome of credulity. 'I don't know much about these financial things, but if you *do* go to the Dordogne won't you have trouble with exchange controls?'

'Some of my best friends work at the Bank of England. No, seriously, I've never been stopped yet at the Customs. All I need is a large suitcase.'

'Or a Swiss bank?'

'Or a Swiss bank.'

'When's the news going to break?'

'In the *Jet* on Monday I hope. It's already written.'

'Supposing the bid isn't confirmed next week.'

'Well, that would be awkward . . .'

'I mean, doesn't it sometimes take a long time to dot the 'I's and cross the 'T's in these bids? I remember Daddy once saying . . .'

'Yes, but if the worst comes to the worst, the beauty of our British capitalist system is that I'll be able to sell all the shares late next week.'

'At the same price?'

'Well, not exactly. Bugger it, why don't you take up law or something? Anybody would think I'd committed a . . .'

'Tarquin!' She accompanied her jibe with a laugh and a slap on the thigh which made me veer towards silly mid-on.

To the background of hooting from the car we nearly hit and several others, I managed to steer the Mini back into the middle lane. We shouldn't take the genuine anxieties of wives or girl friends as personal criticism, but it's difficult not to sometimes. I was already feeling pretty sore that, as a result of the market's reaction to the trade figures, Tring and I had had to take £1.95 as the Terby Holdings current share price in all our calculations. It was psychologically upsetting to say the least. Anyway, the fact that through our bickering we had nearly managed to have a dangerous accident served as a useful bond between us for the rest of the journey, which went without serious emotional incident. Judith did not even complain about the speed of my driving, always a sore point with her. Some months earlier we'd been looking after a suicidal friend of her mother's and took her for a drive over the Sussex Downs. My driving so terrified this forlorn soul that she suddenly decided she wanted to live – a form of death aversion therapy the social services ought to explore.

It was the early hours by the time we arrived in Maentwrog, up there in Merionethshire. And it took a good half hour to find the right track for the cottage. Apart from disturbing a few sleeping cows, nearly driving the Mini into a ditch, and being scared out of our wits by the sound of Welsh speaking owls, we managed the half mile of track without incident. The old Welsh stone farmhouse was circa 1650 and felt like it as I tumbled to the floor on my first contact with the beamed ceiling. 'Not built for the heights of me,' I muttered lamely, in an effort to retrieve my reputation with Judith after an uncomfortable outbreak of swearing.

We slept in a converted granary above the kitchen, with moths fluttering against the window and the old restored beams above giving a sense of occasion to the first successful physical union of Judith Southfields and T. A. R. Quin. In the morning we repeated our triumph. The afternoon was spent loafing about the house and in deck-chairs, with ideas about the ascent of anything other than ourselves never getting beyond the planning stage. We had a good meal in the Italian restaurant at Portmeirion – a semi-oasis in a gastronomic desert – and repaired to the pit. Encouraged by the general trend, I even managed to cook breakfast – eggs, bacon, tomatoes, mushrooms and fried bread before driving off to buy the Sunday papers. There was not a whiff in the papers about the Terby deal – just a letter to the editor of the *Sunday Times* from Terby, drawing attention to his new-found holier-than-thou views on insider dealings and nominee holdings. And, more important, there was nothing of any description which was likely to put ideas into Tring's head about scrapping our piece and following up with something else. It was a great weekend, and at least I caught sight of the mountains.

21

You can get from the Trawsfynydd nuclear power station – the local beauty spot – to London in about four hours if the wind's behind you. Judith and I therefore took a chance and stayed on until the Monday morning, rising with the owls and the larks at 6 a.m.

After taking the Knockin route to Shrewsbury, we managed to survive the Wellington rush hour and were soon on the M6. There's a section of the Knockin route which takes your breath away, being as precipitous as anything one encounters down there on the Italian Riviera; but the feeling was as nothing compared to the suspense as we stopped at the Corley Motorway café, near Coventry, for breakfast and I bought my Monday morning copy of the *Morning Jet*. It was bad enough waiting to see if the piece had gone in as planned, but there was an even worse moment when the guy muttered something about an industrial dispute affecting production in Fleet Street the night before. It turned out that only the *Sun* and the *Mirror* had been hit, and true to form, the old *Jet* couldn't resist shoving in a little subheading: 'The paper you can trust to arrive'.

Now, one of the big laughs in journalism is that you can labour all afternoon to introduce something approaching subtlety into a piece, only to find that the sub-editors, who naturally resent diversions from *War and Peace, Ulysses* and *Penthouse*, ruin everything with an embarrassing headline. Tring, wise to this fact of editorial life, had long since made a practice of discussing the headline with the subs on the phone, to make sure they got it right. That Friday night Tring had gone out of his way to decorate my story with 'ifs', 'buts', and 'possibles', no doubt mindful all the while that if a denial came out from Amalgamated or Terby he could get some mileage out of another powerful piece roaring HOW WRONG THOSE RUMOUR-MONGERS WERE ... What Tring hadn't reckoned with was that during this holiday season, the summer relief sub would listen to his suggestions for the headline, but not pay a blind bit of notice – subs on the rest of the paper being somewhat less respectful of Tring than he liked to believe.

There it was, shouting out loud and clear for all readers in the Corley Motorway cafe and elsewhere: AMALGAMATED TO BID FOR TERBY HOLDINGS. No 'ifs' in that headline; no 'buts'; not even a wet question mark at the end. Here, as far as the rest of the world was concerned, was the great Augustus Tring speaking out loud and clear; and we must not forget what according to my reckoning is the seventy-five per cent of readers who seldom get beyond the headline of most stories.

Oh Jesus. I later heard from Tring's chauffeur – my mate Larry, you recall – that Tring nearly had kittens that morning in the bath – that being his favourite – and some would say most appropriate – place for wallowing in the superficialities of the *Jet*. Apparently Tring charged out of the bathroom without so much as a towel on him – thereby fulfilling the Spanish maid's daydreams in a somewhat dramatic form – and leapt for the telephone, his first thought being not to bollock the sub, but to nail the bearer of the original offending tidings, no less a junior journalistic figure than yours truly. Me. T. A. R. QUIN.

Sitting there a hundred miles away, trying to stomach motorway beverages, I did not hear his call, I must confess; so Mrs Tring and Larry were left to absorb the early morning riot. According to Larry the great man had calmed down by the time they reached Canonbury Square, convincing himself that he had got out of worse scrapes before. In the process he had also arrived firmly at the conclusion that my whole story was up the creek. But the old swindler could not resist saying when passing through the *Evening Jet* City Offices on the way into his own sanctum: 'You chaps look busy. What are you up to? Following up my scoop this morning?'

'Yes Mr Tring,' said a humble practitioner of the old school of financial journalists, a man who knew his place – subservience followed by involuntary retirement. 'The terms have just been announced.'

At this stage Tarquin ex machina appeared on the scene, having got Judith to drop him outside and then bounded up the stairs. I wasn't able to witness the historic delivery of this line, although from all accounts it was delivered with a deft sense of occasion – deadpan. But I was in time for the dénouement. An avid reader of the *Wizard* and *Hotspur* in the old days, I had always wanted to see someone 'stop in his tracks'. Tring did just that, heightening the drama by slipping rather violently on the highly polished floor and enunciating to the office at large the words: 'Christ Almighty.'

I'm afraid that on such occasions I always find it difficult to resist muttering: 'No, just T. A. R. Quin,' but I was interrupted this time by Miss Broadland – an old dear who had been Tring's predecessor's secretary, and who on being fired by Tring ten years ago had continued to hang around the office ever since, making tea for her reluctant boss, and muttering as often as possible, 'I'm very worried about Mr Tring.'

'I do wish Mr Tring would not swear like that,' she said.

By this time Tring had recovered himself, and was walking – I should say strutting – on towards his inner sanctum, muttering – to the *Morning Jet* boys on the other side of the *Evening Jet* partition – 'Morning boys: we've given them something to think about again, I see.'

After the time lag of a few seconds it was now my turn to manifest the physical symptoms of shock, and I turned to old Claude, the guy who had informed Tring. 'They haven't really, have they?'

'Oh yes, Tarquin. It's half shares and half cash. I make it that it puts a value of £2.45 on Terby's shares. Terby's to join the Amalgamated Board as chief executive, and Henry Allan's becoming president. Tring's story was absolutely right – they confirmed it at 9.15 on the tapes, before the Stock Exchange opened.'

TRING's story. I liked that. Never mind. I could hardly see straight by now: £2.45 was nicely above my working assumption of £2.40, and valued my holding of Terby shares at £612,500 minus the £500,000 of nonexistent money with which I'd bought them, leaving £112,500 less the commission. Anyway, I'd clear my £100,000. All I needed to do now was sell them.

22

SELL THEM? My Gawd. It really did hit me now. My planning had been so geared to organising the buying of my aunt's shares that I'd hardly given the disposal of them a second thought. It was one thing to use those stockbrokers – evidently without arousing suspicions – to *buy* the shares. But who would be putting two and two together on their pocket Japanese calculators now but those nine guys whose firms were entrusted, so they thought, with my aunt's business. Nine parties to my crime; not one but nine; good men and true, three-quarters of a jury, no less.

I tried to run over in my mind the conversations I'd had the previous week. I had – I thought – been reasonably adroit in so arranging it that several of those fellows had ended up in the position of advising *me* that my aunt's money should go into Terby Holdings. But was I really in the clear, or was I up to my neck in something else?

The problem lay in trying to remember the exact course of my conversations. I always envy these characters who are supposed to have total recall, because I frequently suffer from the reverse. I accept the analogy of those memory books that one's brain is rather like a library, and there's lots of stuff tucked away that we don't realise. My trouble is that most of my memory books are stored away in the reference section – out of sight and frequently out of mind. Here I was, a few days after one of the most important business days of my life, and I couldn't remember how things had gone.

There was only one thing for it: to get the old librarian out. Retrace your steps Tarquin. Go back to the scene of the crime –

the coffee houses and the pubs, and see if the sight of the walls will remind you of the extent to which you are incriminated, or not.

Thus during Tring's somewhat triumphant conference – he had already managed to convince himself that he alone was responsible for the Terby-Amalgamated scoop – my mind was dwelling pretty heavily on the nastier aspects of my crime, such as would I be found out. Jack Spick was detailed to help Tring with the story on the terms of the takeover, thereby qualifying to hear from the mouth of our old school chum such Terbied words as, 'I see this basically as a marriage of two equal partners', while the old twister's public relations men were busy claiming that Terby himself was worth ninety per cent of any marriage.

After conference I wandered out on a round of the coffee houses and pubs, retracing my steps and, I hoped, my original conversations. The talk with Stephen Hill-Smythe came back fairly easily – without any doubt he had, as it were, snatched the initiative from me in recommending Terby shares, even though it was I who first insinuated the subject into our conversation. The phrase, 'Tarquin, I'm an unabashed bull of Terby's shares', kept whizzing through my mind, and I felt sure that even if Hill-Smythe had any suspicions, he quite obviously had such a long position in Terby's shares (jargon for being so overloaded with one particular stock that you must be hoping for miracles from the share price) that he'd be only too delighted.

Stan Stockton would also be okay. He'd obviously guessed that I knew something, and the glint in his eyes had suggested that he'd be buying *his* line of Terby shares even before he carried out the commission I'd given him for my aunt. Since I'd channelled that extra slice of business through Stan (when John Crampton had advised against buying Terby shares) this meant that I could safely sell the first three tenths of the shares – via Hill-Smythe and Stockton – at once. Similarly, there were three other brokers who had more or less done the recommending *for* me, and I reckoned I could happily ring them up and say my aunt wanted to sell immediately. After all, I'd laid on her losses on War Loan with a trowel; they could hardly object if the old girl wanted to take a quick profit on something that had gone right for her.

But I wasn't so sure about the other four people I'd dealt with. To tell the truth, the smoothness with which my buying orders had been placed was rather going to my head towards the end, and I thought I'd rather overplayed things. In which case there was certainly a danger that those last few brokers might be putting two and two together. I mean, you could hardly get more brazen than buying shares on a Wednesday or Thursday, writing them up in a way which precipitated a takeover announcement, and then selling them immediately.

Or could you? Was I just being a little over-anxious? My little deals were one of many to each of those guys. Would they even remember? The story had gone in very firmly under Tring's by-line; the shares were in my aunt's name . . .

It was all right for brokers themselves when they got inside information. They could buy, sell and take their profit without arousing any suspicions. But the poor old financial journalist who was trying to make a dishonest hundred thousand . . .

To hell with it. Worry about problems when we come to them, as my Greek master would have said. Let's sell the bloody shares.

I rang Stephen Hill-Smythe, and thanked him for the advice he'd given me about Terby's shares. 'You must have known something Stephen,' I said. He, in the way of ninety-five per cent of the adult population presented with a remark like that, said : 'Well, of course, we have our contacts . . . Does your aunt want to take any of her profit now?'

'Not half,' I said. 'The old girl's having paroxysms of delight. Probably put twenty years on her life. She's asked me to sell the lot. By the way, she wants to meet you. Thinks your brain must be paved with gold.'

I winced as I got further into the mire of this absurd routine, and was thankful I couldn't actually see his smirking face. But he bought it all hook line and sinker, and must have made a packet himself out of the deal. I made a mental note to make greater use of S. Hill-Smythe should my aunt require any future dealings.

23

Well, I don't know. Everything always seems to make perfect sense in retrospect; but at the time . . . After all my worries about having been too ingenuous [sic] about my dealings with some of those brokers, the unloading of my aunt's shares went like a dream. Stan Stockton, of course, was delighted with the original tip, and I could hardly get him off the phone. The guys I'd been ultra-careful with smelt no rats whatsoever. And the three or four whose suspicions I'd definitely aroused with my sudden order followed by confirmation in the *Jet* – they didn't care a damn. Why? Because the whole lot of them had been wondering for ages why I didn't dabble in the market; each thought his relationship with me was something special, in the sense that he thought he was the only broker I would wish to use; and they all came to the conclusion off their own bat that my unseemly haste meant I must know something, and know something really big. As I said earlier in this book, there are no flies on guys whose business it is to make money. I'm reminded of the occasion we heard on the tapes that the government was going to abolish the distinction between dollars for buying houses abroad and dollars for other overseas investment. There used to be separate markets in these and at the time the premium on property dollars was way above the ordinary dollar premium. Jack Spick, being essentially naïve about the capitalist system he was intent on destroying, rang up a merchant bank and asked them what would happen if the two markets were merged. 'Hold on a minute,' said the fellow at the other end, and Jack overheard him say into an internal phone, 'Edwards, sell all our property dollars.'

Then the fellow resumed: 'Now what was that you were saying Mr Spick?'

To get back to the point: a man's word is his bond in the City of London and four brokers who'd made a nice turn out of the Terby deal were not going to be too scrupulous about the enormous weight of circumstantial evidence surrounding the *Jet* story and my own dealings in the market. As one of them laughed over the phone when I dropped my selling order in: 'Your aunt is singularly well informed, Tarquin. I should love to meet her.'

So there we were, just like that. In case any of them was fussy, I'd kept in reserve the idea of getting Judith – or her mother – to ring up and confirm the selling order in a female voice; but it wasn't necessary. We had bought, my aunt and I, with money we hadn't got; and we had sold, my aunt and I, without even having to take delivery of the share certificates in Terby Holdings. All done within the official account period, and the cheques representing the difference – £100,000 plus – were due to be sent within ten days or so after the end of the week. What a splendid system the London capital market is; so convenient for the likes of me: socialists turned liberal capitalists, men who have a natural right to benefit from the system we don't really want to destroy.

The odd thing, though, was the fact that with all those guys in on the act, the Terby share price had kept so low on the Friday. Granted, the trade figures had depressed the whole market, but the upward pressure on Terby Holdings was enormous. Somebody – somebodies, as the Rogan kids would have said – must have been doing an awful lot of selling. John Crampton, for one – the character who had firmly put me off buying Terby's shares on the grounds that the essentially shady nature of his empire was beginning to catch up on him, as demonstrated by Terby's sudden conversion to attacking all the practices he was associated with, such as insider dealings, the use of nominee holdings etc.

John Crampton: yes, he must be furious at having sold out. His buying was the main reason why Jim Parsons had been able to use his favourite phrase 'a good two way market' in his reference to Terby Holdings in the Saturday paper's market report.

John Crampton. Yes, he must be in trouble, I thought, as from my desk that Monday afternoon I completed the last of my selling orders on the telephone, having made it clear in each case that my aunt had asked me to act entirely on her behalf, and that the cheques should be made out in *my* name – which produced not a murmur of dissent from our honest brokers. John Crampton, yes he must be a bit sore. Let's just hope he doesn't put two and two together and cut up rough. Anyway, I picked up the phone again to ring Judith with suggestions for the night's celebration, when a hand landed firmly on my shoulder. I looked up. Holy Godfathers. Great Mother Machree. John Crampton. My Catholic conscience needed no more. 'I'll come quietly,' I quipped, and got to my feet.

24

A few words about Crampton. I earlier made the mistake of imply-
ing that Crampton was an orthodox City figure. It depends, as
Professor Joad would have said, what you mean. A man who can
conceive the sort of plan Crampton outlined to me in the comfort
of his Brompton Square house that night can hardly be considered
one hundred per cent orthodox, even by the standards of the
financial world. No, he just seemed orthodox – until the chain of
events which started when he laid his hand on my shoulder that
afternoon.

Crampton came from those well-known despisers of money,
the lower reaches of the British aristocracy. However much the
supercilious gentlemen dissemble, there's no getting away from
the fact that money made them, whether their ancestors filched
it from the peasants a few centuries ago, or more recently from
the backs of nineteenth century wage slaves (on which subject,
incidentally, Marx is less convincing than Engels, not to say less
readable).

Sorry, this isn't meant to be a sermon – I'm the last one in a
position to preach. All I want to get across about the Cramptons
of this world is that money made them and it's money they spend
their lives trying to preserve. When the money runs out, they'll
resort to anything, preferring, on balance, hell later to the poor-
house now. No Pascallian wagers for *them*.

Crampton was in his early forties, and in many respects a
junior version of that high-class villain who has already cropped
up in this story – Lord Brachan. I meekly followed him out of
the *Jet* office into the street, where he hailed a cab, mentioned

his number in Brompton Square, and buried himself in the *Evening Standard* as if I wasn't there.

When we got out of the cab he led me up to his first-floor drawing room. Those houses are perfectly proportioned, but unlike some of the Georgian houses I was familiar with in Islington, this was also elegantly furnished. Not a sign of the children's gum boots and nappies which bring the lines of your average Islington house into social perspective. Pictures and prints beautifully hung all the way up the stairs; the drawing room itself a sort of identikit dream of how most of my friends would like to furnish such places if they weren't totally stretched paying off the mortgage.

Only, if anything this was too perfect. Why, there didn't even seem to be a wife in sight to disturb the fastidious proportions of that L-shaped first floor, let alone a child. Crampton managed to make a momentary wince into a long-suffering gesture as I tripped on one of his many oriental rugs and spilled a drop of Tio Pepe. For the first time I noticed his mannerism of readjusting the cuffs of his well striped shirt almost every five seconds. Then it struck me. Crampton was very punctilious. Crampton was queer.

'You should be more careful with people's property Tarquin. Persian wool and . . . sherry don't mix.'

'I . . .'

'No matter. Drink up and have another. We are going to see a lot of each other. I like to look after my house guests.'

'Can I just ring my girl friend?'

'You can try. Perhaps you are an electronic genius. It's been out of order for days.'

'Now look here Crampton. Just because . . .'

'. . . just because you've nearly ruined me you're going to have to do what I say Tarquin. I need your help.'

'What do you mean nearly ruined you?'

'You know perfectly well what I mean.'

'Look, cut the cramp – I mean crap – Crampton. The shares you were advising people to sell have gone up. It happens every day. So what?'

'What would you make of the position of somebody who had sold vast quantities of Terby Holdings short, and is now faced with the problem of buying them back at this inflated price?'

Oh ho. So *that* was it. While I'd been busy buying Terby's shares on credit waiting for them to go up, Crampton had been flogging a lot more than his clients actually had. He was now faced with the delightful prospect of buying Terby shares to meet his commitments at the new ruling price of around £2.45. The reverse of my own operations. Instead of collecting the difference he was losing it. No wonder he'd been advising me, a potentially influential financial journalist, not to buy the bloody things for my aunt the previous week.

I now regretted, not for the first time, my natural tendency towards flippancy. Not having been able to resist the remark, 'I'll come quietly', I seemed to have embarked on a course of submission to Crampton's will, by meekly accompanying him to his house without any protestations, tacitly admitting my crime.

The mannered poise of some homosexuals is an act they can only sustain between frequent intervals. Crampton suddenly got up from his chair, stubbed out his cigarette (which was in a long slender holder, of course) and stamped about the room like a child that had lost its toy. Whatever nasty plan Crampton had in store, he was at this stage more interested in crying on the shoulder of the man who had – nearly – ruined him.

'Tarquin, you know I told you Terby's spivvery was catching up on him – that day when I advised you not to buy his shares?'

'Something of the sort. Yes?'

'At the time I had good reason to believe an exposé of Terby's outfit was going to appear in one of the Sunday papers.'

'Poor you. And?'

'It was held up by the lawyers.'

'Meanwhile you'd started selling Terby Holdings short?'

'Exactly.'

'Then came my story, and the confirmation from Amalgamated Industrial.'

'Precisely.'

'And even if their exposé does have an effect on the deal, it could not possibly appear before next Sunday?'

He nodded sourly.

'Meanwhile, the Stock Exchange closes on Friday, and you've got to buy the Terby shares before then?'

Again, a sombre nod.

'Oh Crampton, you *are* in a bad way.'

He suddenly rushed across the room and grabbed me by the lapels.

'Don't you laugh. Unless you help me now, I'm going to the Press Council, the Stock Exchange Council, the Takeover Panel and the police if necessary. And I'm going to tell them the connection between our own sharedealing and the *Jet* story this morning would repay investigation.'

'Look, for God's sake. All I've done is print the news about something which was going to be announced anyway.'

'Yes, but not necessarily this week. Anyway, that's irrelevant. The point is, Tarquin, that I have a plan to retrieve the situation, but I need an accomplice.'

As he said this, he showed distinct signs of recovering his more casual demeanour. 'Preferably,' he went on, 'an accomplice I have a hold over – whom I can ruin if he does not co-operate.'

'Steady, Crampton,' I said, regaining something of my own occasional calm. 'Hasn't it occurred to you that I may have a hold over you? That the Stock Exchange Council and so on might be interested in investigating the background to your *own* recent dealings?'

'Pointless, Tarquin. Such a tit-for-tat struggle would finish us both.'

He wandered over to the window, ostensibly showing an intense interest in somebody's attempts to park a car. Then, in a decidedly nastier tone, he resumed:

'We have a choice, you and I, Tarquin. Either we ruin each other; or we co-operate. I have no idea how much you've made out of your little operation, but I can offer you the incentive of more if you go along with my plan. But if you don't . . .'

Having nothing to lose but my apprehension, I said nothing. He poured us another drink.

'You will appreciate, Tarquin, that I have got to get Terby's share price down before Friday.'

'Yes, I think that's one of the things I'm prepared to appreciate this evening.'

'There is only one way of doing that.'

'Oh,' I replied. 'What, pray, is that?'

'Simple. Remove him.'

I suffered hypochondriacal palpitations immediately. We were now leaping into the megalomania stakes, were we? My new found liberation from squeamishness about money was one thing, but this was getting dangerous.

'What? *Kill* him? You must be joking. Don't be so bloody stupid Crampton.'

'And you don't rush to premature conclusions Tarquin. No, no, dear boy. Nothing so distasteful. We merely remove him from the scene for a few days – that's all.'

'What, you mean . . . kidnap him?'

Crampton clapped his hands ironically. 'Oh, well done Tarquin. You're getting quite bright in your old age. I might even be tempted to award you an alpha for that.'

'I see. With the disappearance of the man whose so-called talents are the reason for Amalgamated's inflated bid, the price for Terby Holdings comes tumbling down.'

'Precisely, my dear Watson. You can empty your head of Agatha Christie and Lord Peter Wimsey, Tarquin. As Oscar Wilde would have said, a murder in this case would be *too* extravagant. A kidnapping will surely suffice.'

'So for your purposes all that matters is that the word should get round that Terby is missing?'

'Through the good offices of your very own media, Tarquin. And if . . . if people like to conclude that he *is* dead – well, that would be all to the good.'

Crampton waved his cigarette holder nonchalantly and went

on. 'I spent a profitable hour earlier this afternoon with a friend from 'C' division. He more or less worked out my plan for me. I told him I was writing a detective story. Our policemen are so wonderful.'

I hadn't agreed yet, but it was pretty obvious which way things were going. Whatever financial incentive Crampton was offering didn't matter, except as grist to the mill. There were two reasons for agreeing to participate – one, to preserve the ill-gotten gains I'd already made, by stopping Crampton from informing on me; and two, the sheer attraction, at the basest human level, of being a party to the kidnapping of my life-long enemy, the egregious Derek Terby.

'Just to help you make up your mind, Tarquin, I ought to tell you that I took the trouble this morning to sell a lot of Terby Holdings shares in your name. Having got the price up, you now have a direct interest in getting it down again. Don't you think?'

'You mean . . .'

'Yes, Tarquin, luckily – as you know – a man's word is still his bond in the City of London. As far as I'm concerned, you telephoned me today and sold a large line of Terby shares. The instruction is already recorded on the files. And I have the good fortune to work for a firm whose record in these matters is impeccable . . .'

'You bastard, Crampton.'

'. . . whereas your own recent record, Tarquin.'

'You cunt.'

'Tut, tut. Such language in one so young.'

'Now wait a minute Crampton.'

He made a fey, dismissive gesture with his cigarette holder, then looked at his watch.

'I can certainly wait Tarquin. In fact I can wait ten hours. But I want you back here sharp at 6 a.m. tomorrow.'

I began to mutter inanely. He cut me short. 'Go away Tarquin. I have arrangements to make. See you at six.'

After Crampton had dismissed me I remembered that I'd left the Mini at London Wall. On the bus back I began to think the situation over in the hope of convincing myself that matters were not yet completely out of hand. Not for one second would I have believed that story about his selling Terby shares in my name at the inflated price – as an incentive for me to assist him to get them down. No, I would not have believed that if, on my way out of his door, Crampton had not thrust a piece of paper into my hand which I now read:

'We have sold, subject to the rules and regulations of the Stock Exchange, by order and for account of T. A. R. Quin, Terby Holdings £1 ordinary shares

    Quantity 50,000
    Price £2.40
    Consideration £120,000

This was the usual wording of a stockbroker's contract note, and it was on Crampton's firm's official paper. I could double check with one of his clerks the following morning, but there was no reason to believe it wasn't genuine. The first thing that struck me was Crampton's implied contempt for my whole operation. He had no idea that I had already made £100,000 out of my dealings, and obviously regarded this piece of paper as a real incentive to myself. Yet even if Terby's shares halved as a result of his disappearance, by buying at the lower price I would only stand to make just over half what I had already achieved.

Did I say 'only'? I really was becoming complacent about my misdeeds. As the bus approached Piccadilly Circus I began to look at things another way. Crampton wasn't offering me an alternative, but an increment of anything up to fifty per cent, say, on the £100,000 I'd already made. I preferred to think that he was bluffing about turning me over for investigation by the Takeover Panel and that lot. He knew I had as big a hold over him as he had on me. My deliberations were interrupted by the sight of a minor demonstration which held up the bus for a few minutes as we approached Trafalgar Square. Then I remembered the venom with which he had said: 'Either we ruin each other; or we co-operate.'

25

'Sometimes I feel my talents are wasted. I'd make an excellent detective.'

It was 6.30 a.m. in Crampton's house the following morning – the sort of time when you can appreciate the glories of early blue sky and sunlight in London without being put off by throng or traffic. Unfortunately it was raining and I was a nervous wreck. I'd spent the rest of the previous evening with Judith, and filled her in on the events of the day. She had certainly inherited Mr Southfields' own somewhat suppressed streak of adventure: after agreeing that there was no alternative but to play along with Crampton she said: 'Perhaps I've been watching too many television serials Tarquin, but I'm going to follow you and give Daddy frequent bulletins as to where we are.' We had got more and more excited about the whole prospect as the evening went on. With the aid of an alarm call, we surfaced at six and staggered into the 'his' and 'hers' faded blue jeans and jacket which were all the rage at the time. Then Judith took me from Godfrey Street to Brompton Square in the Mini, and drove round the corner to a double yellow line in Brompton Road to await developments.

Crampton opened the door, and immediately looked at his watch.

'Our transport arrangements have been finalised, and our destination is fixed. I reconnoitred yesterday evening. It's now 6.33 and Terby's due to leave London airport at 9 a.m. We are going,' he paused to emphasise the point by stubbing out his cigarette in a delicate manner, 'we are going to divert his journey at 7.45 a.m.'

As Crampton stood there – a little taller than my own six foot two, with his black silk dressing gown and those pinched cheek bones – I reflected that he saw himself as a mixture of James Bond and Sherlock Holmes. He could have his daydreams, I thought, provided he didn't regard me as the queer version of Pussy Galore.

'I shall retire to my dressing room for five minutes, Tarquin. Please look after the furniture.'

I idly inspected his bookshelves. They were stuffed with first editions, guaranteed to bring out the covert covetousness in any non-philistine. But I couldn't really concentrate on my own envy. All right. Judith and I had agreed the previous evening that if the kidnapping went well, and the price of Terby Holdings fell 'on Terby's disappearance' (I could just see Jim Parsons writing the market report), then neither Crampton nor I would have any interest in betraying the other. It was all very clear cut – just a pity that last night's Dutch courage had given way to a pretty jittery feeling this morning. Was I really doing this for the extra money? Or because I was scared that Crampton would wreck my own coup? One could see how people living on their nerves turned into alcoholics. It was 6.40 a.m. and I needed a drink. Crampton was still upstairs, so I went over to the drinks cupboard to review the possibilities. An unopened bottle of Courvoisier; just the job.

Ever had trouble removing that strange blend of plastic and tinfoil they wrap around the tops of booze bottles these days? After my nervous fingers had eventually managed to grip the thing, I immediately broke my thumbnail. Like any hypochondriac, I went through several seconds of feeling as if the end of the world was imminent. No good biting the wretched tinfoil – that would finally demolish the ailing filling system in my teeth. Then I remembered the little girl-guide's knife Judith had given me. The bottle opened, I now, with great prescience, felt the need for a glass. Crampton – of course – had a beautiful collection of Georgian glass in a cabinet; I tried to open it; it was locked. Hey ho. I raised the bare bottle to my mouth and was in mid-swig when my effete host, having tripped in daintily from nowhere, tapped me on the shoulder and said: 'So *soon* Tarquin? You are not the man I took you for.'

'Well, I, er . . . Jesus Christ.'

I was stopped in my incoherent verbal tracks by the sight of Crampton. Gone was the meticulous dresser. Abandoned was the vision of James Bond. In his place was a figure with dirty brown desert boots; the hard-wearing sort of blue jeans which look as if they have never seen better days; one of those ghastly Marks and Spencer bri-nylon objects which are neither shirts nor jumpers (it was green); and a garish Indiacraft scarf whose colours included egg yolk which was rather obviously genuine.

Now despite the unseemliness of the hour – it was still only a quarter to seven – my mind had succeeded in churning up a few questions for Crampton – such as why on earth was Terby due to fly from London airport in the middle of a big takeover bid? Where the hell was he going? And in any case how did Crampton know? But in circumstances like these we are easily diverted. The first thing I asked Crampton was why he was in this get-up.

'Dear dear. I see I have aroused your suspicions Tarquin. But I think you'll find that I shall arouse nobody else's. I have deliberately got myself up like the typical harassed, appallingly dressed fathers I observe all over the place in these days of emancipated women.'

Better watch your typically harassed poovish mannerisms, I muttered. Then, aloud: 'Driving the typically harassed father's Lamborghini I take it?'

'Dear me, Tarquin. When *will* you grant me credit for some subtlety. Look outside.'

He pointed to an orange and cream Volkswagen bus, the sort of family wagon which haunts all those areas of London such as Hampstead and Islington where the middle classes are desperately trying to reverse the downward slope in the population trend.

'There you are. Our ideal family bus. Nobody will look twice at it.'

'Wouldn't it look more impressive if it contained your ideal family?'

Crampton didn't answer for a second, but his manner gave me the impression he, at least, thought he had thought of everything. Then he said: 'Sit down Tarquin, while my manservant deals with your moustache.'

His personal Philippino more or less emerged from the wall. 'Hey, waid a minute,' I heard myself say Bogart-style.

'Now you just go to the bathroom with Angus [sic] and you'll come to no harm,' said Crampton. 'Your hair is a splendid length for our purposes, but your moustache is none too wifely. You'll look a different man in a few moments.'

Eh? What? Well, obviously I didn't like the idea, but as long as I could play along with Crampton I felt I had to. And at least Angus was a dab hand with the scissors and razor. Off it came.

'Excellent,' said Crampton a few minutes later. 'But your spectacles are aggressively masculine. We'll have to remove those while we're in the car.'

I didn't like the sound of that, and convinced Crampton that my spare pair of lensed sun-glasses with light metal frames would look well on his wife.

'What about my bra,' I asked.

Crampton hesitated for a while. 'No, it would make you look like a female impersonator. You've got the right lean hollow look of today's mums. Right, now all we need are the toys and the children,' he said. 'Angus would you like to go downstairs and load the car.'

Well, it was the most bizarre kidnapping party I'm ever likely to participate in. While Crampton and I watched from the first-floor window, young Angus trooped out from the basement to load the car: first with a selection of teddy bears and cars, and secondly with two little boys aged about two and a half and one and a half, each in a pramtop which fitted into the back of the van. Then he produced an au pair girl.

'I have lodgers in the basement,' Crampton explained. 'A wife who needs a lie-in. Because the poor girl has a title, she was hounded by your egregious colleagues in the press throughout the divorce and custody proceedings. My offer to take the au pair girl and the kids out for a couple of hours came like manna from Heaven. Let's see now. It's 7 a.m. Our little family is complete. A less suspicious looking party it would be hard to contemplate. Let's go.'

26

The rain proved to be a light shower. It had almost stopped, and the setting for the day's criminal activities was a newly washed London. You could hardly see the early morning sun, and the larks were in good voice. 'Now,' said Crampton as we turned into Brompton Road, 'I'd better put you in the picture. Terby is due to fly to Edinburgh at 9 a.m. The reason is that one of the largest shareholders in Amalgamated Industrial is a Scottish insurance company, and they are kicking up a hell of a fuss about this whole business of Amalgamated bidding for Terby Holdings – a fuss, incidentally, which would have made you a good story in the *Jet*, if only you had had the nous to discover it yourself Tarquin. Anyway, Terby is trying to persuade those shrewd Scottish investment analysts that he's worth what the Amalgamated Board says he is.

'How do you know all this?' I asked. 'And why the hell, if it is true, do you have to go through all this kidnapping nonsense. I could write the story up in the *Jet*, and that alone would be enough to get Terby's shares down sharply.'

'I should be careful what *you* write in the *Jet* from now on, young man. Anyway, you're *so* naïve. I have known people devote a whole day to briefing young financial journalists like yourself on some scoop, only to find that their editor refuses to use the story or there's not enough space, or something.'

'Yes but . . .'

'I certainly thought of asking you to write that story Tarquin. Every little helps. But we've got to be absolutely certain the bloody shares go down. One insurance company's views don't carry enough weight. Who knows? There's probably some fool within a hundred yards of us' – we had now turned into Fulham Road – 'who would snap up any Amalgamated or Terby share he could get his hands on.'

'Okay. But . . .'

'To cut a long story short, I have good contact with this insurance company, and you may deduce it is no coincidence that both they and myself have recently been bears of Terby's shares. As to Terby's movements this morning . . . well, behind the absurd image hacks like yourself have built up around him lies the suburban little man that Terby really is. I took the precaution last night of telephoning Mrs Terby and posing as your friend Augustus Tring. People are so trusting on the telephone. Damn these bloody traffic lights. Always red – it doesn't matter whether Fulham Road is chock-a-block or empty. Ah that's better. Now where was I?'

'With trusting people on the telephone.'

'Yes, well we had a lovely chat, with Mrs Terby looking out of the window intermittently to see whether your charming friend Derek was turning into the drive. So nice that Derek did not believe in working in the evenings. Such a pity that he would miss the school open day, because he had to fly to Edinburgh, driving himself to the airport at 7.45 . . .'

'I see.'

So. Mr Southfields having been dismissed as chauffeur, Terby was off by himself in the Jaguar. Meanwhile, here we were, this crazy party in a Volkswagen bus, off to intercept him, chaperoned by two kids and an au pair girl who didn't speak English in the back. How? Where?

One always has – at least I always have – a sense of abandonment of responsibility as a passenger in somebody else's car. On this occasion my feeling of being a passenger in another's virility symbol was compounded by the fact that, minus my moustache, I was in any case meant to be posing as Crampton's wife. Mine, I felt, on this occasion, was definitely the submissive role. How and where to waylay Terby I left to Crampton to tell me in his own time – which would be half an hour at most.

In the absence of further information, what was intriguing me was whether Crampton had arranged for somebody else to do the initial dirty work, or our little party was actually going to waylay Terby itself. As we drove on down Fulham Road and across Putney Bridge, I began to suspect the latter. We were heading straight for Terby's house which, Terby having come up in the world – a full three hundred feet from down there in the nether regions of Cottenham Park – was situated in Wimbledon Parkside. Facing the Common, and near what the showbiz colonisers of my former territory had chosen to christen 'the village', the Terby residence stood well within its own grounds – a 'businessman's mansion' (in Roy Jenkins' memorable phrase) if ever there was one.

My heart beat faster, sank, and generally behaved in cravenlike detective-story fashion as we passed Tibbett's Corner and drove along Parkside. The Wimbledon Common windmill came within sight on our right – no more than a quarter of a mile from 'Chez Terby' [sic] and still no elucidation from Crampton. I looked at my watch: 7.20, some twenty-five minutes before Terby was meant to be driving off solo to the airport.

In the back the kids were now out of their pramtops sitting around the table you can rig up in those vans, playing with their Teddies. The au pair girl was dividing her interest between them and a magazine. Crampton saw me looking round and said: 'I thought twice about bringing them, but if something goes wrong we do need them. No policeman would suspect our little family.'

He stopped the car at the end of the road that leads to the Windmill.

'Now, she can get out and take the kids for a walk in the pushchair, and we'll pick them up a few minutes after we get Terby.'

'What *about* Terby? Won't the kids notice him? Won't he notice the kids? For Christ's sake Crampton, what are you playing at?'

'Oh Terby won't notice anything. He'll be rendered unconscious by my dope gun.'

If it had been possible to walk up and down while being safety-belted to the passenger seat I should have done so. I economised on the histrionics, however:

'So *that's* what your friend from 'C' Division advised. Honestly, Crampton, I thought you were a James Bond fan, but it strikes me you're living in the world of Dan Dare. I think I'll take the District Line myself. I could be back at my girl friend's for breakfast.'

Good wifely talk, this.

'You'll do no such thing,' Crampton shouted.

I looked at my watch. It was now 7.25. A less smooth operation than seemed apparent at 7.20. Crampton looking somewhat ruffled.

Then, from the rear of the van, came the voice – I should say voices – of sanity.

'I wanna pee pee,' said one child.

'I wanna cuddle,' said the other.

'Please, stoop ze car,' suggested our au pair girl of the hour.

'Ze car ees already stopped,' bellowed Crampton.

27

Well, many was the game of cops, robbers, cowboys, and Indians I had played on Wimbledon Common in my time, although kidnapping was unfashionable in those halcyon days. Here we were for real, but it had never been quite as farcical as this, even when little Derek Terby, aged eleven, was one of the players.

The au pair girl put two-and-a-half-year-old Marcus on one potty; I, my experience of living next to the Rogans turning up trumps, deftly sited one-and-a-half-year old Alexander. Crampton – 'it was never like this when I was in the Guards' – paced up and down, rubbing his hands distractedly on his jeans.

The iron rule about putting kids on potties is that they want to get off when you're not in a hurry but stay put when you are. It was now 7.29, and the lads looked set for a day's sit-on, the au pair crouching as well in order to give young Alexander his protracted cuddle.

They say the abandonment of national service was the beginning of the nation's decline, but with leadership such as Crampton was showing I wonder. I myself am a great one for panicking in times of minor crisis but keeping relatively cool when the roof shows signs of collapsing. Sheer terror keeps me cool, I find.

'Come on Crampton, let's just drive on. This is what she's paid for.'

I closed the sliding door those vans have on the near side, and climbed in. Crampton got back into the driver's seat. 'It's seven thirty Crampton. I suggest you fill me in fast on our next move.'

We had about three hundred yards to go before reaching

Terby's place, with the houses on our left, and the Common on our right. There was little sign of early morning walkers or horsemen, and Parkside is not exactly brimming with pedestrians even in rush hour. I noticed that one or two of the old houses had been demolished since my day to make way for the neo-georgian estates of neo-villagers; but either side of 'Chez Terby' were houses similar to his – large 1930s style places, of the sort which allowed the *News of the World* and suchlike to indulge their fancy for the phrase 'known locally as millionaires' row'.

Crampton stopped the car outside 'Chez Terby'. He was now back in command. 'I had a good look round here late last night,' he said. 'There are two entrances to the drive. Terby's Jaguar is outside the front door, pointing in the direction of this exit. We'll be blocking his way when he will already be a good seventy yards away from his wife and farewells, and completely out of sight of the house.'

I nodded. This was more like it. I was being dominated by my husband again.

It was 7.34. Eleven minutes to go – provided Terby hadn't decided to leave early. We were about as prepared for that contingency as the CIA appears to have been in all those bungled operations you read about. Now *I* was getting nervy. I thought of Tring, still no doubt congratulating himself on *his* scoop about Terby. I thought of Lord Brachan, the link man in the Amalgamated/Terby deal, restorer – until this morning, we hoped, of Blizzards' ailing fortunes. I thought of Jack Spick, planning the overthrow of capitalism from the safety of Surrey; of Mrs Cordoba, part-time wife to Terby's partner George Cordoba; of Mr and Mrs Southfields, calmly breakfasting on the south downs, safely in and out of Terby's shares. I thought of their daughter Judith, my girl friend – Judith: partner to my thoughts, observer of my crime, who came flashing past this instant in the Mini, absolutely on cue.

Judith, anxiously trailing and watching over me – could I really go to the Dordogne without her? Could I really, back to reality, *get* to the bloody Dordogne. What *was* I doing, here in the middle of Crampton's escapade?

These thoughts, those of a drowning bravery, absorbed a full ten seconds of the world's time. Then Harold Wilson interrupted them: 'Tarquin, put this on.'

Crampton handed me an Edward Heath face mask, having put the Wilson one on himself while I was daydreaming. Then he started talking as though we had all the time in the world to spare.

'Tarquin, when I was in Korea, I learnt that the secret of an ambush operation was fifty per cent good planning and fifty per cent calm improvisation.'

Jesus, what a time for reminiscences. 7.36 – nine minutes to go – or less: he could hardly have synchronised watches with Terby.

'Now,' he went on, 'this mask will disguise your face. Has Terby ever heard your voice?'

'Only about five million times.'

'Seriously?'

'Seriously.'

'Right, we conduct the rest of the operation in silence. You are to bend down and examine the front near-side wheel with an interest you have seldom shown in a car before. I'll hide in the bushes.'

Never having been a boy scout myself, I was beginning to warm to Crampton's somewhat belated show of leadership. I donned the mask and crouched down at the wheel. Crampton's last instructions were: 'Whatever sounds you hear, just stay there until you hear me start the engine. Then hop in without a word. I shall have to talk to Terby. Don't be surprised at my accent.'

The first sound I heard was the creaking of my knees as I attempted to crouch down.

It was 7.38.

After an interminable wait of at least four minutes, I heard the excessively punctual sound of Terby's car starting up – several minutes ahead of our time. There were muffled sounds of farewells, then came the crunching of gravel and the grinding of low gears in a hurry, interspersed with the occasional short skid. It was the unmistakeable sound of a car reversing ...

Korea was never like this, I thought, as I heard Crampton curse and dash past me, speeding along the pavement to intercept Terby at the other entrance.

Now, if there was one thing missing from our commissioned officer's fifty per cent planning and fifty per cent improvisation routine at this juncture, it was revised instructions to yours truly. The whole point of Crampton's ambush was that the Volkswagen would be blocking the Jaguar's path. Well, even an impractical buffoon like myself can occasionally get the message. I jumped into the van, thought of doing a 'U' turn but rejected the idea because, although nothing was in sight, Parkside is a high-speed deathtrap and we were near a deceptive bend where something could emerge from nowhere. So, I just had to reverse the van along the pavement – some thirty-five yards.

I backed the thing along in zig-zag fashion, my only guide being the view of the kerb and one lamp-post through the mirrors. The cream rear bumper was a great help, easily visible, but at one point, in order to avoid the lamp-post, I zigged (or zagged) into the garden wall. This was with about five yards to go, when I assumed Crampton was already at the entrance Terby was heading for.

Crampton later told me that by now he was hidden in the bushes, wondering whether he dare run out on to the gravel, since it sounded as though Terby had taken the Jaguar from zero to sixty in about two and a half seconds as he rounded the bend. 'Will the sight of Harold Wilson make the bugger drive straight into me or veer into the bushes?' is the thought Crampton recalled running through his mind.

I managed to drive the Volkswagen forward a yard, get it clear of the wall and reverse the remaining few yards just in time. We were blocking Terby's way; there was a screech of brakes, and the rear of Terby's car skidded to the right, into the bushes. This left Terby almost facing the bush opposite, swearing volubly. At which point Crampton emerged from that same bush, wearing his mask.

Well, to suffer one shock in your hurry to get to the airport is bad enough ... I swear I almost felt sorry for Terby at that moment, as his already startled gaze alighted on the grotesque figure of Crampton in jeans, jumper and Harold Wilson mask, carrying an object which Terby could be forgiven for thinking was a gun.

It *was* a gun: an American 'Mace' dope gun, as Crampton later informed me with some glee. Banned in England, they were being used at the time in the States by the police to deal with rioters – as in Mayor Daley's Chicago, for example. The gases knock someone out for about a minute – sufficient for our increasingly robust-looking Guards officer to handcuff Terby, tie a hood over his head, and give him a fireman's lift into the front of the van.

The inside designs of those vans vary a lot. This one had a passage between front and rear, affording enough room for Crampton to lay the five-foot-six-inch Terby down, with his head between the two front seats.

It was now time for amateur dramatics. I of course had not moved from the driving seat since reversing the van. Crampton now sat in the passenger seat, with his right hand poised menacingly round Terby's neck. The whole operation, from firing the gun to Crampton's placing his hand there, had taken no more than forty seconds.

Crampton then spoke in a voice which was a passable imitation of Mike Yarwood doing Wilson. 'Right, let's go and pick up the others.'

There were already signs that Terby was, as they say, 'coming round'. Crampton leaned over him, and in the same voice said: 'Terby, if you say or attempt to do *anything*, your short repulsive life will come to a swift end. If, on the other hand, you co-operate, you need have no fears.'

Crampton had probably been rehearsing this remark all night.

It was a pity for him that he mistimed it. Terby was obviously in no state to take in a word, but continued to say and attempt quite a lot. Crampton held him down; I drove back to where we had left the girl and the kids, and ushered them into the back. Terby's ravings were becoming comprehensible, but they consisted, to my disappointment, of nothing more original than: 'Who are you? Where am I? What's this all about?'

At which point Crampton repeated his warning and Terby took more heed.

It was still only 7.55. For variety I drove a different way back, down Somerset Road, past the All England Tennis Courts, through Southfields, Wandsworth and Battersea, and across one of the bridges. In the back, ignorant of the drama they had partly witnessed, the two little boys were happily beating each other up with cars, while the au pair – wrapped up in a not-so-real-life crime story – intervened from time to time when things became a bit too violent. Terby kept quiet. Throughout this return journey I, his old school enemy, said not a word. With Terby under cover, as it were, we removed our masks for the return journey. Nothing could have been more calculated to arouse the suspicions of the fuzz than the sight of Harold Wilson and Edward Heath travelling together. So far, so good, I thought, as we turned into Brompton Square at 8.20 a.m.

28

'I wery hungry,' said the two-and-a-half-year-old.

'Why vewy hungi,' echoed the one-and-a-half-year-old.

The voice of Crampton/Wilson/Yarwood said: 'Right, take them in T . . . .' He stopped just in time and did not actually say my name. I had noticed Crampton's habit of repeating the name of the person he was speaking to in almost every sentence. Such little things are the stuff of detective work.

'Right, take them in,' he corrected himself in time. 'They're expected. I'll stay here with our guest. Then come straight back.'

All we needed now, I thought, was for Terby himself to whine, 'I wanna pee pee' – but we were spared that. I opened the sliding door of the van and helped the au pair to take the kids back into the house. We were met at the door by friend Angus, and a lady who was presumably Crampton's basement lodger, having had a lie-in for a change, and some respite from the early morning kids. She was quite tall, fair haired and . . . no, such details are not necessarily relevant to my story at this stage.

Well it hadn't exactly been a great outing for those kids; I felt slightly sorry for them at the time, but my experience since then suggests it doesn't matter at that age whether they go for a boring car ride or fly to the moon in the early morning – as long as they're fed before 9 a.m. The other thing which surprised me was the docility and total lack of curiosity about this strange outing shown by the au pair. Here again, however, greater experience of au pairs has taught me that the surprising thing is when they show an interest in anything other than Soho clubs.

When I returned to the van, Crampton indicated that he

wanted me to take over the vigil of holding Terby's head down with one hand, and pressing a pistol into his chest with the other. While I did so he scrawled out a note: DRIVE ACROSS ANY OF THE BRIDGES AND HEAD FOR THE A2/M2: WE'RE GOING TO FOLKE-STONE.

I took the van through Eaton Square, down Belgrave Road, across Vauxhall Bridge and out to the A2 via Camberwell Green, Peckham and Blackheath. That was a good three-quarters of an hour of ghastly London driving. But thanks to the earlier shower of rain the atmosphere was not quite as heavy as it is on those sunny dry days when London is muffled by a haze of traffic fumes. Terby's main contribution was a subdued repetition of 'I must cancel my meeting . . . I must cancel my meeting', to which Crampton, in his Yarwood/Wilson voice kept replying, 'Your meeting has cancelled itself brother.'

Once we were clear of London, the rest of the journey went very smoothly. We covered the sixty-five miles or so in about an hour and twenty minutes, with no subterfuges from Terby about needing a pee or anything like that. I drove the way I knew, turning off the A2 at Canterbury and continuing the pilgrimage via Stone Street to join the A20 just to the west of Folkestone.

On the way into Folkestone there is a quiet little suburb called Cheriton – quiet that is, unless they start fooling around with the Channel tunnel again, the entrance being between the Cheriton houses and the southern side of the North Downs. But at that stage the tunnel entrance was only a gleam in the planners' eye – I mention it simply because it was projected for the end of the little semi-detached road which Crampton now directed me to-wards – Surrenden Road.

With its roadside trees, and its gardens in full summer bloom, Surrenden Road looked like your typical Acacia Avenue, and the least likely venue on earth for a pair of nefarious kidnappers such as J. Crampton and T. A. R. Quin. I drove half-way down, and Harold Wilson's voice asked me to stop at the right side of a semi-detached pair on our right. Town and terrace dweller that I then was, I looked at him gormlessly, wondering just how we were going to unload the hooded figure of Derek Terby on to those innocent flagstones in broad daylight.

Our retired Guards subaltern had a higher Edward de Bono rating.

'Get out. Open the gates. Open the garage doors. And drive right in.'

I managed this delicate operation with only one minor hitch – we knocked over a green plastic watering can, but it didn't disturb the neighbours.

'Right now,' (still forbearing to use his favourite verbal mannerism and say, 'Right now Tarquin), 'get out, squeeze your way round to my side, and you will see a side door to the garage. Open it, then open the side door to the house, which will be facing you, with this key.'

I did so and found myself in the kitchen. Meanwhile I had visions, based on falling asleep during too many midnight movies, of our having to carry a kicking and screaming Terby out of the van. But all that happened was that I heard Crampton saying: 'Stand up, Terby. Keep your hood on and walk straight ahead. You can take roughly three paces, then be careful of a six-inch step up into the house. If you co-operate neither you nor the contents of this gun will be disturbed.'

It was all remarkably easy. Nothing like the farce and near cock-up we'd had over grabbing Terby in the first place. And I for one had had sufficient experience of Terby's cravenness over the years – he was too timid even to jump over a vaulting horse – that I was pretty sure he would co-operate with Crampton all the way along the line his precious skin was stretched.

Looking back I still cannot believe how easy it was to transfer Terby to that little suburban house. The side-door to the garage was perfect. It was shielded from the road by a high side-gate to the garden. And at the end of the cricket-pitch length garden was a fence leading to a deserted playing field. The house to the immediate right of our temporary abode had no windows in the side wall other than frosted glass for the lavatory. We had not been followed, nor even observed from a helicopter. We had got away with it – so far. At least, I say we had not been followed. We had been pursued by Judith, my protectress, and the Mini had been continually in view in the driving mirror all the way down.

Crampton disappeared with Terby upstairs, and asked me to make some Nescafé. He returned in a matter of minutes, sporting a complacent smile.

'A pleasant drive, Tarquin, if I may say so. That's the most difficult part of the operation over successfully.'

'What now, brown cow?' I said, handing him his coffee.

Crampton looked at his watch. 'Let's see. It's half past ten. You're going to be late for work Tarquin. You'd better get moving: there is a tolerable train service from Folkestone to London – about seventy-five minutes plus ten minutes walk from here to the station.'

Well, the thought had already occurred to me that it would look a bit suspicious if Terby *and* the journalist who'd written up the takeover story suddenly disappeared at the same time. Even more disturbing than Jack Spick telling his mother he and I were going on holiday together, you might say. But the great thing about the *Jet* was that you could, at a pinch, always take the morning off without too much trouble – Tring himself set a pretty good lead in these matters.

'What about you, Crampton?' I asked.

'I've arranged to take a few days' holdiay. Come to sunny Folkestone.'

As he said this, I thought how absurdly inappropriate the kidnapping gear of jeans, desert boots and Marks and Sparks nylon shirt looked on the normally almost foppish Crampton. Then something rather more disconcerting occurred to me: 'Jesus Christ – my moustache . . .'

'You'll just have to grow it again Tarquin. I must say, you look almost attractive without it.' So saying, he patted me on the cheek. 'What an excellent wife you have been.'

They try to say extreme distaste for queers is a sign you're not too sure of your own sexual status. That's a load of psychiatric double-talk that's never worried me – I think. Nevertheless, even in this absurd situation, with Terby somewhere upstairs and not a chance that Crampton would be making any passes, I found myself instinctively stepping backwards – on to the pedal bin, as it happened.

'Well, er, see you around,' I said, plunging towards the door.

'Yes, around 9 p.m. here,' replied Crampton forcefully. 'I took the precaution of bringing a picnic for Terby and me to have at midday, but I want you to bring back enough food to keep us going for a few days. I need hardly add that some wine for dinner would not go amiss.'

29

Like most perfectly fit hypochondriacs, I spend three-quarters of my time feeling like the man in those 'Are you one degree under?' advertisements. That 6 a.m. rise had been a bit hairy. As I walked down Surrenden Road towards the main road I felt like having a good kip.

In my dozy state I momentarily forgot about Judith, who had been parked down the road, waiting in the Mini. She drew along-side and I slid gratefully into the passenger seat.

'Well, Bulldog, how's it going?' she laughed.

'He's got Terby somewhere in the top of the house. I'm to go to work this afternoon and return tonight with food and drink.'

'He'll soon be issuing you with battalion standing orders. I take it you want me to buy the food.'

'It would help. I'll deal with the wine.'

'I noticed you'd lost your moustache Tarquin the moment you stepped out of Brompton Square. What on earth happened?'

I explained Crampton's idea about our looking like a married couple with the kids in the back to allay suspicions.

When Judith had stopped laughing she said: 'That's about the craziest scheme I've heard for years. Honestly, Tarquin, no one would mistake you for a female from even five hundred yards.'

That was reassuring after Crampton's unpleasant little joke flirtation in the kitchen.

'Apart from my moustache, I can't understand why Crampton should have wanted the au pair girl and the kids for such a short time.'

'Oh, that's understandable. It was a good precaution to take just in case you bumped into the police on the Wimbledon trip. Just imagine trying to bring that party all the way down here though.'

'I suppose so. The next question is: when does the alarm go off?'

'While you've been up to your tricks I've had the car radio on all the time. There's been nothing on the news yet.'

'Terby was meant to be flying to Edinburgh. I imagine they won't know until he fails to turn up there.'

'Darling, you're forgetting something. Cast your mind back to Terby's drive. Didn't you hoodlums leave a little something there – one abandoned Jaguar, to be precise?'

'Yes, well . . . I suppose somebody *might* notice that,' I replied in my favourite recovery-situation voice, a feeble imitation of my old Greek master.

Since neither of us had had any breakfast, we stopped for a snack at a small transport cafe near Maidstone. There was a newspaper kiosk next door, and this gave us our first opportunity to look at the papers. Tring had chosen to write the follow-up story on the Amalgamated/Terby deal with the aid of Jack Spick and as I expected, the result was beyond parody, with a huge headline proclaiming 'I TOLD YOU SO', a photograph of the strong Monday morning headline which had so embarrassed Tring at the time ('AMALGAMATED TO BID FOR TERBY HOLDINGS'), and a story which began: 'They don't call us the JET SET for nothing. To all those readers who have followed my advice and bought Terby Holdings shares in the past three years I say: "Fortune is merry, and in this mood will give us anything." Carry on Derek Terby and good luck. The slumbering Goliaths of British industry need more Davids like you. Lead on, Macduff . . .' etc. etc.

Was this the Tring who had described Terby in my hearing as 'a jumped-up little spiv' less than a week ago? It was. This was the Tring, by appointment purveyor of forgettable words to the masses, riding on the glory of the moment, after – judging by today's choice of quotation – a particularly good lunch even by his own standards.

I glanced through the other papers. All the interpretation was based on the easy bull market assumptions of the moment, glib so-called analysis boiling down to the general message that if Great Britain Limited was run by dynamos such as our Derek, the country's economic problems would sink to the bottom of the North Sea.

Even Lex in the *Financial Times* was vaguely bullish about the deal – from what one could make out of the convoluted jargon they used in that column at the time, before the editor told them to start writing in English. As for the business gossip columns, written largely by people who didn't know Terby from Lord Brachan, they demonstrated once again that sycophancy is far from being a dying art.

We got to London at about half past twelve. There was no point in heading for the *Jet* office – the lunch three hours would have started promptly at 12.05 – so we went to Godfrey Street, where we'd spent the previous night and I'd left my suit.

The cleaning lady had been and gone, leaving in a neat pile a batch of letters addressed to me. In the general excitement I'd overlooked the fact that the brokers' contract notes confirming my *sales* of Terby Holdings at the higher price would also be coming to my temporary accommodation address.

Excellent. The selling deals were struck as near, on average, the £2.45 price ruling for most of Monday as to make virtually no difference to my calculation that the clear profit was comfortably above £100,000. In a couple of weeks I should receive the cheques and, hey presto, Dordognewards we will go.

The house had an area of concrete at the back which would have been described as a 'yard' in Bradford but was very definitely a patio here. My friends the wine-dark Steadmans had been trying to grow vines in this area, and the general effect of shrubbery and whitewashed walls was too tempting to miss on what was now a very hot day, with the atmosphere still benefiting from the early morning rain.

I warned the reader at the beginning of this account that the porn-hungry had better moisten their chops in other pastures. I've had a one-track mind during most of this book, and the track has been money. But if I add to this description the fact that the high walls around the yard meant that at midday you were overlooked only by hot sun, you will guess what I'm leading up to. It was a setting too good to miss. Judith popped out to the King's Road to buy some bread, pâté, cheese and a bottle of dry white bubbly wine. Yours truly just sat there in the garden patiently waiting. He had to. He couldn't move. The problem was whether his beloved would get back in time. I have to confess she didn't, from the point of view of her satisfaction first time in.

'Don't worry darling,' I quipped, 'there'll come another time.'

There did. The great thing about what they call premature ejaculation is that it can be followed by something more mature. But that's not all. I suppose it serves you right if you make love to the background of Radio Four, but the next ejaculation came to us as the most premature of all. No, we were not completing a hat-trick in the sex olympics. We were listening to the breathless voice of the late William Hardcastle, with the World at One. 'A dramatic development in the takeover bid for Amalgamated Industrial. Derek Terby, the man the City was expecting to run the proposed Amalgamated/Terby combine, is reported missing. Later in the World at One we interview Mrs Terby on the extraordinary circumstances surrounding her husband's disappearance. In Vietnam . . .'

30

Joan Terby didn't have much to say. While Judith and I lay barely picnicking – entwined, oh so entwined, in each other's limbs – poor old Joan (I remember her well: she'd been at the local convent) mumbled on with the stock responses to the stock questions.

'I can't believe it . . . we said goodbye to him . . . he drove away, perfectly happy . . . the children and I went back to finish breakfast . . . then at eight fifteen, when I was driving them to school, we came across Derek's car, abandoned in the drive . . . I just can't . . . oh . . .'

'It's all right Joan, he's perfectly safe,' I said to the somewhat unreceptive Roberts 707 she was speaking from. 'It won't be long dear.'

It was perhaps unfortunate that I should have simultaneously chosen to advance my pâté-greased hand along Judith's right leg, which had for the last few minutes been resting contentedly on my left thigh.

'Tarquin, have you *no* sensitivity? Can't you spare *some* sympathy for the woman. Imagine what she must be going through.'

From what I recalled of Joan Terby (née Simmons), her concern for Derek's life would come a poor second to the question of whether or not he had packed his pyjamas. But this was not the time to compound one infelicity with another.

'Sorry darling.'

'I should bloody well think so. Pig.'

The brief contempt was enough to make us miss whatever enlightenment the World at One team could throw on Terby's disappearance at this stage. (Wasn't I just dying to know? Wasn't I just full of wonderment as to where he might be? Wasn't I even just a little interested in whether the police *knew* where he might be?) The key words coming over the air, however, amounted to no more than 'mysterious disappearance', 'Police and family baffled'. I caught a reference to the share price falling, but missed the crucial figures. So many personal quarrels seem to take place when all you're trying to do is listen to the wireless ...

Judith had meanwhile stalked into the house. She re-emerged about five minutes later, bathed and clothed.

'Come on. Get dressed and I'll give you a lift to the office. I should have thought the earlier you get there the better. Someone may need you to help them with their enquiries.'

Judith dropped me by the Bank of England and went off to organise the shopping for the strange household in Folkestone we were returning to that night. When I got back to the office it was only 2.10 – a time when the *Evening Jet* staff was hard at work between editions, but the rest of the fellows on the *Morning Jet* were still at lunch. And would be, for at least another hour – two in the case of Jim Parsons.

I wandered into Tring's inner sanctum, to pass the time of day with his secretary Susanna. She would know what, if any, had been the repercussions of Terby's disappearance on the market and, for that matter, on the office.

Susanna was tall and thin, permanently tanned by the sun in summer and various lotions in winter. She had voluptuous lips, which were always particularly enticing when one found her in Tring's office all by herself. On such occasions she would mix flirtatious movements of face and body with reverential references to her boring boy friend. It took me some time to realise that those references were equally provocative in the scheme of things.

She teased me about the disappearance of my moustache, making me forget the purpose of my visit. Then she broke off: 'Oh, I forgot. The chief crime reporter's been on from the Fleet Street office. Wants to speak to *anybody* in the City office about Terby. You can call him on extension 436.'

Oh boy. This was too good an opportunity to miss. 'Get him for me Susanna will you,' I said with Tring-like authority.

The chief crime reporter was called Harry White. I'd met him once, a seasoned Fleet Street journalist, half as old as time, with the wounds from forty years' boozing much in evidence around the nasal capillaries.

'I like old Harry,' I said while she was dialling, 'but I doubt whether I'll be able to help him very much.'

My quid pro quo from Harry for telling him some of what he needed to know about Terby – a poisonously objective account – was a promise that he would tell me everything he had gathered from the fuzz on and off the record about their theories – purely as a matter of interest, of course.

It was obvious that at this stage the police hadn't got a clue, literally. The British cops find it difficult enough to arrive at the conclusion that someone has been kidnapped, let alone actually handle a kidnapping case. As a CID character told me many months later: 'Kidnapping's just not Scotland Yard's scene.' As for motives: well, there was I hanging on every reaction Harry might have to those elements in the Amalgamated/Terby takeover deal I was prepared to explain to him, and I don't think the thought that there could be a link even crossed his mind.

The only financial angle which had occurred either to the police or to our chief crime reporter was the obvious one – that Terby was a rich man, in demand by a rich company, and that therefore, if he really had been kidnapped, there would eventually be a ransom demand.

'Look Tarquin,' Harry explained, 'can you blame the police for taking it easy? They get thousands of cases a year where the relations think somebody's dead or kidnapped, and all the guy's done is gone for a walk.'

The market was at this stage as sceptical as the police about the whole business. I'd motioned to Susanna to get me the latest tapes, and all that had happened was a 10p drop in the shares of Terby Holdings from £2.45 to £2.35. Lots of talk about confused reports re Terby's whereabouts, but nothing firm.

According to Harry White, the police spent the first hour after Joan Terby had sounded the alarm trying to calm her. The first theory was that Terby had at the last minute panicked about the time, car parking problems at the airport etc, and abandoned the car in favour of a passing taxi. Between 8.20 a.m. – when alerted by Mrs T. – and 11.30 a.m. – by which time it was clear Terby had definitely *not* turned up for his meeting with the insurance company in Edinburgh – the only fingers lifted by the cops belonged to the shaking right hand of Mrs T.

'Well, I'm watching this one, but I've also got a big bank robbery on my plate this afternoon,' said Harry. 'If you or your financial friends hear anything, or have any bright ideas as to Terby's whereabouts, give me a buzz, Tarquin. Cheers, old chap.'

No sooner had I put down the phone than the switchboard girl, knowing I was ensconced in Tring's office, put another call straight through to me. It was Crampton, speaking from Terby's whereabouts.

'What's the number? I'll ring you straight back,' I almost yelled, terrified at the thought that the switchboard girl would be listening in to this dynamic conversation. I then rang Crampton from a corner of the outer office, on one of the private lines the *Jet* had conveniently installed for the personal lives of its staff.

'I've just talked to our chief crime reporter. It's fantastic. The police haven't got a clue what's happened. They'll never trace you,' I said with an overdose of the criminal beginner's enthusiasm.

'Fuck off,' said Crampton. 'I'm worried Tarquin. I've just talked to my office, and the share price is only down to £2.35.'

'Well, that's something.'

'Something? It's derisory. How long will it take the police to catch on?'

I was enjoying this. Crampton was shrieking with nervousness. I expounded a combination of Harry White's and my own views on the speed with which the British police move in a kidnapping case. 'Aren't you deriving any intellectual pleasure from the brilliance of your technique?' I ventured.

'Fuck off' (again). 'We must have a serious conference about this tonight Tarquin. You will be back at nine won't you?'

'Yes darling,' I said.

'Yes *what*?'

'See you later.'

I liked the fact that Crampton's unflappability was only skin deep. No doubt Nelson's was the same. As for me, well the reader will know by now that I don't make any exceptional claims for myself in this matter.

The office gradually began to fill up with various casualties of the City's pubs and restaurants. Jim Parsons reeled in with a market rumour that Terby had at the last minute flown to America to persuade some important holders of Amalgamated Industrial stock in New York of the wisdom of the Amalgamated/Terby Holdings merger. The deputy financial editor said he'd heard rumours about Terby's health, and maybe the poor fellow had suffered a loss of memory or something.

Jack Spick, who'd by now been landed with the whole Terby/ Amalgamated story because it was a week of heavy economic news for me, had of course decided to concoct a theory that Terby – all the time we'd known him – was a secret Communist who had chosen this embarrassing moment for western capitalism to defect. Jack's elaboration of this view was interrupted by Augustus Tring, who'd slipped quietly in during the general shouting. 'If I get any more theories like that from you, Jack my lad, you can find yourself a job on *Socialist Worker* where you belong.'

'They don't pay enough,' said someone (not Jack).

'Anyway, enough of this. Write me a decent story on the status of Terby's shares *ex* Terby,' said Tring – a statement which confirmed, much as I hate to admit it, the view that in spite of everything I held against him, Tring was on top of his job after all.

But it didn't even occur to the ever suspicious Tring that there might be a more direct causal connection between Terby's disappearance and market manoeuvrings; all he offered was : 'I bet Terby's just playing silly buggers to cause a stir. Little squit.'

The afternoon passed more or less without incident. I tried to jazz up a 'no change in industrial production' item into something slightly less tedious sounding. Jack Spick spent a long time on the line to various board members of Amalgamated Industrial and Terby Holdings, who were playing it fairly straight, finally managing to convince him they didn't know where Terby was, but that Moscow was one of the less likely locations. The market began to lose some of its nerves during the afternoon in the continued absence of firm news, and Terby Holdings closed 20p down at £2.25, still way, way, above the price at which Crampton, my partner in crime, had sold them short.

31

Half an hour before I was due to meet Judith downstairs at the *Jet* office, I received a telephone call.

'Is that Mr Quin?'

'Yes.'

'I don't know if you remember me. My name is Lord Brachan.'

'Yes, Lord Brachan.' Three bags full, Lord Brachan.

'I was wondering,' after a second or two in the depths, his voice rose into that familiar high-pitched whine affected by the not-so-distressed gentlefolk. 'I was wondering whether you might not have time to call upon me at Blizzards.'

'Certainly Lord Brachan. When? May I ask in what connection?'

'I'd rather not say on the telephone, but it is a matter of some importance to myself. Can you come round now?'

I was somewhat staggered by the easy availability of His Lordship, and found myself saying: 'Yes, fine.'

I was ushered in by the same flunkey as on the previous occasion. Brachan rose, languid as ever, trying to give the impression mine was the only appointment of the day, and that we had all the time in the world.

'Tarquin. Come in, dear boy.' (I could hardly go out: the flunkey was still firmly planted in the doorway.) 'Have some tea. Milk? Sugar? No. Sit down. I'll attend to it. Now, how are you? What have you been *doing*?'

I started to answer these questions as if they had really been asked. He could hardly have been less interested.

'Tarquin, I sometimes wonder – don't you? – about the ethics of the City. I have spent most of my working life in politics. I know what hard work is. But these people' – he made a dismissive gesture towards the Stock Exchange, which was only too visible from his elegant seventeenth-century window – 'these people seem to think the world owes them a living.'

'Yes, I suppose I see what you . . .'

'I read an interview the other day with one of our well-known socialist millionaires. He said he couldn't help making money; he had this magic touch; but that the way he made money in the City did nobody any harm.'

'Yes . . .'

'But if somebody makes himself a quick £100,000 or so, that, according to the perhaps too elementary economic textbooks I was brought up on, that gives him a claim on the country's resources that most other people won't have in their lifetime.'

'Well, yes, I suppose . . .'

I shifted uneasily, as they say. Was my uncomfortable feeling as he said 'quick £100,000 or so' just paranoia? Or did the old rogue know something?

'Interesting view of socialism, don't you think?'

'Well, yes, but . . .'

'This City's full of people making a quick £100,000, Tarquin,' (like Your Lordship's good self, I thought). 'I feel sorry for these pathetic train and bank robbers. Such gangs as – what are they called? The Krays?'

I shifted uncomfortably again. Brachan was by now leaning over his desk, his long neck poised like a swan's for take off.

'Those poor gentlemen are in prison, Tarquin. But the real criminals are all in the City of London. You presumably read *Private Eye*? Perhaps you' – a really sideways look at this point – 'perhaps you write it. Yet, how big is the City's fraud squad? For years one could count them on one's fingers. No wonder the real criminals never get caught.'

Not bad, I thought. Just the sort of lecture I should have enjoyed delivering myself in those not so distant days – about two weeks ago – before I decided to join the real criminals and do it their way. As for *Private Eye* ... how would the Slicker column ever have got off the ground without contributions from the likes of Jack Spick and me?

Brachan leaned back, evidently pleased with the effect he was having. But why? How did he know? Or did he?

'I was talking about you the other day to Derek Terby. He's one of our clients now. He said you were an old friend of his – how much he liked you. What a pity Terby seems to have disappeared. It could be very embarrassing for Blizzards. Very embarrassing indeed.'

'Yes. Er. I suppose it could.'

Brachan just sat looking at me now. No more banter. Nothing After what seemed like thirty-six hours but may have been no more than thirty-six seconds he stood up, came round the desk to proffer a leaden hand, without taking his eyes off mine, and said: 'Good day to you Tarquin. How nice of you to have called.'

I walked back to the office, puzzling over this strange interlude, and made a quick check call to Harry White.

'No news. The cops had a good look at the gravel in the drive. They've established that Terby's car skidded violently, but they don't know why. They're really not very interested, Tarquin. And even if he doesn't materialise tomorrow they won't be able to follow anything up until there is a ransom demand. Meanwhile they're half-heartedly watching the ports.'

Judith had stocked the Mini with food for Crampton and Terby, plus ourselves. We picked up a case of booze at a City wine bar, and headed for Folkestone, one of the ports the police were no doubt watching half-heartedly.

I briefly told Judith about the events of the afternoon. She, wifelike, said: 'You know, Tarquin, I've been thinking. We must have been drunk last night. I'm becoming more and more uneasy about this Crampton business. And, I don't really believe he has a hold over you if you pull out of the whole thing now. Why don't you just leave him to it?'

'Because he knows exactly what I've been up to and he could ruin me if he told the police.'

'I think your conscience is over-guilty.'

'Why?'

'Well it was you and Daddy who pieced the story together. You didn't exactly act on inside information given to you in the course of your job, did you?'

(I may say that although Judith knew broadly how the story had been got together, I'd had to alter names and circumstances when it came to Mrs Cordoba's role in the detection work.)

'It was partly in my job. Look, you don't understand, I've got no conscience about it. That's why I did it. My only worry is being found out. All I've done with my own coup is a variation on what goes on all the time in the bloody City.'

'I should think you've got more chance of being found out if you go on with this kidnapping business than if you stop now. Anyway, it sounds as if this Lord Brachan knows something already. He must have been giving you a discreet hint.'

We hardly spoke for the rest of the journey. I had of course been completely caught up in the excitement of the Crampton affair. But the more I thought about what Judith said, the more I began to wonder. Perhaps Brachan did know something. Apart from anything else, we were in the ridiculous situation where the kidnapping seemed to have worked, and the real problem was to make sure the world *knew* Terby had been kidnapped. That was, if we could make ourselves heard above the noise which would undoubtedly, on past experience, be made by all the nuts and hoaxers in the next two days. It was Tuesday night, and the Stock Exchange account would close on Friday. Unless the market got the message and Terby Holdings really did fall heavily in response to Terby's disappearance, it would be too late from Crampton's point of view.

When we got to Surrenden Road Judith refused point blank to come in.

'I'll wait outside. I should think Crampton's feeling pretty jittery by now. If he sees that there's another person involved he'll explode.'

I made two journeys to the doorstep – one with the food and

one with the drink – and rang the bell. Crampton was in the same incongruous clothes he'd been wearing that morning. The hand holding the cigarette-holder was none too steady. 'God I need a drink Tarquin. Come in.'

I opened some wine and Crampton organised the food. We each had two large whiskies while these preparations were going on, and by tacit agreement did not talk seriously until we started eating. He was much more relaxed now, back to the mannered poise.

'We'll give Terby his food later, Tarquin. I've got him tied to a bed upstairs, and he's frightened out of his wits. He's so scared that I haven't even had to put a gag on his mouth. He really seems to believe I'll kill him if he yelps.'

'That doesn't surprise me. He was no Kojak at school.'

The morning's events had been too precipitate for me to satisfy my natural curiosity as to whose house Terby's temporary prison was. 'It belongs to an actor friend of mine, Tarquin. *Anybody* can enter and inhabit an actor's house without arousing the faintest suspicion – even in Folkestone.'

We were eating in the kitchen, and the proceedings had assumed the casual nature of one of those old-style City lunches where the real topics didn't crop up until the port. After the second bottle of wine I felt the urge to explore the house.

'Do take your mask, Tarquin, there's a good boy. Since you know Terby so well it would be singularly rash of you to expose yourself. He's in the main bedroom, overlooking the front garden. Such sacrifices I make for my guests.'

Even allowing for the calming effect of mother alcohol, I was curious at how relaxed Crampton had suddenly become. I had a pee in the downstairs loo, and then wandered around. Any reader familiar with children's modern bedtime stories will know what I mean when I say it was the sort of house Topsy and Tim and Janet and John would have felt at home in. Front sitting room with latticed windows; living room at the back; four bedrooms upstairs; and the sort of staircase which has several landings in a small space; on which landings there were traces of recent infant revelry.

Infant revelry indeed. Games on Wimbledon Common with little Derek Terby. My Edward Heath mask well to the fore, I stole into the front bedroom to take a look at Terby. Fastened to the bed, he was just able to move his neck.

'Oh my God. Not another bloody politician. Or are you the same man?'

I shook my head, but said nothing, knowing Terby would guess any version of my suburban voice a mile away, and vice versa. I thought Terby's attitude remarkably truculent for the man I remembered. I almost admired it. A few years as a paper tycoon had done wonders for him.

As I went downstairs Terby's voice came after me: 'What are all those lovely smells? What about a bit of food for me? If you keep starving me like this my body will be worth nothing.'

That was typical Terby. Finance came into every sentence. Crampton said: 'I'd better go and spoon-feed him. Help yourself to the port.'

While Crampton was upstairs, I thought back over Terby's career. As he went from success to success, people kept writing articles asking: what makes him tick? The real answer was: nothing special. Terby was wound up in his mother's womb, and programmed to keep ticking for seventy odd years. In a way his success was the product of his greyness. Being slung out of school for poor progress in the sixth form had a big effect on him and he became the hardest-working student at the local technical college. He swatted along the accountancy path, and in his spare time developed an interest in the racing pages. Various systems with two-year-olds brought him a measure of success, until those well-known risk-takers, the bookmaking profession, began refusing to accept his bets.

Then, as he told Jack Spick during one of those lunches they'd had some years earlier, when Terby was still unknown in the City, he discovered the Stock Exchange during the boom years of the sixties. 'Jack,' he had said, 'for anyone who is any good at gambling the stock market is a revelation. It's like betting on horses with sure knowledge that you can get most of your money back whatever happens.'

Terby had done his betting with, literally, chunks of companies. He had dived in and out of other people's nest eggs like a cuckoo. As the going got harder, however, and the stock market became at best a static investment, Terby relied more and more on sheer wheeler-dealing, talking up the price of shares he wanted to sell and making the best use (i.e. personal profit) out of every bit of inside information he could get his hands on. Just the sort of method I had now used myself so successfully with his own shares . . .

Talking of which, Crampton now came down the stairs, having fed the hand we hoped was feeding us.

He sat down: 'Pass the port please, Tarquin.' He sipped his drink and remained silent for a few minutes. Then: 'When the hell is the price of Terby's shares really going to tumble?'

As Crampton said these words I thought I detected an unpleasant glint in his eye. Then he picked up his glass, threw it with a violent gesture on to the floor and shouted: 'I don't care. I don't care. Because if the price doesn't go down any further, it doesn't matter any more. There's something else we can do.'

He came round and grabbed me by the lapels. I experienced one of my voluntary palpitations.

'Don't you see? The fact that we've got away with the kidnapping so easily means we can change our plans. We can.' (Crampton pushed me violently across the room, just for added emphasis.) 'We can kill the bugger.'

'Yes, well . . .' Issuing this sort of threat in a suburban Folkestone kitchen, Crampton looked somewhat more menacing than in the refined safety of Brompton Square. To ram home the shock to my system he then produced a revolver and began aiming it at imaginary targets around the room. 'Just see what happens to the bloody share price then . . . we can' – he emitted a burst of maniacal laughter – 'we can *shoot* the share price down . . .'

Not a joke in the best of taste, I thought, as Crampton doubled up with mirth. I wondered whether the hysteria was not beginning to disturb the neighbours; they, however, were so used to Hamlet, Macbeth and God knows what murderous bellows being rehearsed in that actors' establishment that they appear to have taken all this in their stride. But it was certainly beginning to disturb one member of the audience – a voice from the gallery; one Derek Terby; who yelled: 'I'll do anything you want.'

32

We amateur diplomatists have to consider the balance of power
– to skirt round the quicksands before they skirt round us. Like
many people, I recover quickly in emergencies, while being inclined to get into a flat spin if asked to pass the butter. I had at
least kept calm during the past ten seconds; but as Terby's
pathetic shout came down the stairs I realised that I had stupidly
missed a big opportunity, because it would have been perfectly
easy to part Crampton from his gun while the bastard was doubled
up with laughter at his own joke.

It was now a case of playing for more time, and trying to calm
Crampton. Another – preferably less dramatic – diversion was
needed, to give me a few seconds to think.

'What's that noise in the garden?' I said.

'What noise?' Crampton swung round jumpily, hesitating over
whether to point the gun at me or the door, and settling for the
ninety degree arc which took in both targets.

'A rustling of some sort. Probably a cat. But don't you think
you ought to go and investigate?'

I must say, I thought that was a pretty good move. The mere
suggestion that I might want to assume some of the authority
in our strange alliance evoked just the sort of perverse reaction
from Crampton that I needed.

'No, you go, Tarquin. If it's the police, then they can have
you first. Go on; you go.'

My first thought as I prowled around that empty garden noisily
enough for Crampton to hear, but not so as to disturb the neighbours into thinking that there were villains around – my first

thought was how easy it would be for me to escape. Judith was parked somewhere in Surrenden Road; even if it might be risky to go out via the side door, all I had to do was hop over one of the garden walls and make a quick exit via the neighbours.

But my instinct told me that I was in no real danger from Crampton myself – at least, not yet. He had trusted me sufficiently to believe I would return that evening. He needed me for help in seeing that whatever message he wanted to get across to the media actually made it. But the gun . . . I was desperately trying to think what the look in Crampton's eyes reminded me of as he had brandished that weapon. Of course . . . Crampton had mentioned earlier that he had served in the Korean war. My own national service – I was one of the last to get caught, right at the end of the fifties – had never taken me beyond Catterick Race Course. But I had got to know several regular officers who had been out in Korea. The remoteness of that war had left a mark of ruthlessness on some of those involved. They didn't feel they were fighting for their country, and there was a sort of corruption about one or two of them that one normally associates with mercenaries.

Indeed, some of them went on to hit the headlines as mercenaries in Africa. At this stage of my deliberations in that dark garden, I tripped over a child's tricycle. Concern for sore shins momentarily absorbed all my limited span of attention. Then I thought that if I wandered about the garden much longer Crampton might start getting worried, and down would go my existing store of dubious credits with him. On the way back to the kitchen door I caught the scent of a rose while managing to scratch my face badly on the accompanying thorns.

The conclusion I was coming to in this obstacle course around the gardens of outer Folkestone was that Crampton, in his present mood, called to mind only too vividly one of the nastier veterans of the Korean war I had known. In spite of his fastidious veneer I could not be sure that Crampton had not been equally corrupted by that war in his attitude to human life. If the prospect of one's own death concentrates the mind wonderfully, then the prospect of someone else's at least distils the prejudices. To think that I had gone around for years to all and sundry describing little Derek Terby as my life-long enemy. What rubbish. God, how we exaggerate our minor irritations. My feelings towards poor Terby were certainly moving rapidly into perspective now.

Any repugnant emotions Terby might have evoked in me over the years were as nothing in the light of the real sense of evil being generated by Crampton – my partner in crime, the only man outside the Southfields family who knew about *my* crime, the man who threatened to make me an accessory after the fact to the crime of killing Derek Terby. By comparison with the mad Crampton, Terby was a boon companion. There was no question that I had to stick by Terby now, while doing all in my power to humour Crampton.

Crampton. What was the silly bugger up to now? Out of the kitchen loud and clear came the opening lines of the *Marriage of Figaro* – 'Cinque Dieci ... etc.' Totally hooked on Mozart as I am, I'm still one of those guys who didn't listen to their mothers saying 'There's a time and place for everything' for nothing.

Jeepers creepers, I asked myself. Does he want the Folkestone police only, or the Dover Patrol as well? I re-entered the kitchen to find my advice already anticipated. Crampton was staggering about the kitchen, a bottle of scotch none too steady in his right hand, muttering, for my benefit, 'S'all right, s'all right. Some fellah banging on a wall. I turned it down, turned it down ...'

'Are we looking for the CIA or something?' I asked. 'Do you want to attract every copper in the south of England?'

'S'all righ, s'all righ,' he gurgled.

'S'all righ indeed,' I thought to myself. I couldn't help being reminded of the Italian garage mechanic who used to service the little Fiat I had before the Mini. You'd give him a catalogue of items needing attention, and without listening to a word he'd say: 'S'all righ ... I feex.' If you'd told him Italy had been taken over by the Moon, he'd have said 'S'all righ, I feex.'

Now, although I'd decided – before the operatic interlude began – that I was very definitely on Terby's side from now on, I hadn't had much time to work out where we went from there. I certainly wasn't prepared for Crampton's next move, however – a blend of the vertical and the horizontal. He just sank to the floor and lay in a heap.

We'd certainly had quite a lot to drink, and I suppose my entanglements with tricycles and rose bushes in the garden were at least consistent with the theory that by now I may not have been entirely sober myself. But Crampton really was smashed; and although the whisky bottle he was still clutching spoke eloquently for itself, it now clicked with me that Crampton must already have been very drunk indeed when he started waving that gun around.

I had practised my fireman's lift many a time on the Rogan children, but the dead-drunk weight of Crampton was in a different league. I staggered through to the sitting room, and lowered my egregious colleague on to the sofa. I then lowered myself on to a nearby armchair, to recover.

The *Figaro* was still on in the background, but not so loud as to provoke more banging on the walls from the neighbours. It's a great country that can bang on the wall because of the music, yet ignore the accompanying murder threats.

The temptation now was to leave Crampton to it. As Judith had said, the longer this business went on, the more likely we were to get caught. Much better to abandon town with the £100,000-plus that I'd already made, and descend on the Dordogne with my Judith – always being prepared to return in years to come and serve my fellow citizens, financed by the interest on my ill-gotten gains.

Problem number one, however, was that I couldn't leave the country until I'd picked up the readies, and it would be several weeks before the proceeds fed through the stockbroking system.

Problem number two was Terby. With Crampton in this condition I could free him instantly. But. But. If I rescued Terby and deserted Crampton, the latter's ominous warning that 'we could both ruin each other' would be very much apropos. With his coup, not to say his bank balance, in ruins, Crampton would be very likely to strew my path to the Dordogne with his own particular brand of vengeance.

I took a careful look at my criminal partner, and decided he was likely to lie there in his catatonic stupor for some hours. Then I went back to the kitchen and resorted to the time-honoured method of drenching one's face in cold water, in the hope of reviving the diminishing band of brain-cells.

I realised, lapping more and more of Folkestone's municipal water supply over my moustache-less face, that the change of my attitude towards Terby was not just the result of Crampton's murder threat. My sordid pleasure (up to a point, Lord Brachan) in having been an accomplice to the kidnapping had served its own cathartic purpose. So had the fact that my entire coup had been conducted in the shares of Terby's own company. It was as good a way as any of dealing with my ethical grounds for complaint at Terby's style and methods. A psychological block had been removed; I bore Terby no ill-will, and wanted to do him no more harm.

I was also helped in this decision by the fact that, try as I would, I could not relegate the session with Lord Brachan earlier in the evening to the back of my mind.

How or why Brachan could know anything about Crampton's operation was beyond me. But he and Blizzards certainly had a lot at stake, and our extraordinary interview was obviously a classic example of the City Establishment's famous method of communicating, on the really important matters, in 'nods' and 'winks'.

So I was in a position where I wanted to save Terby's skin without losing my own (physically or financially). If Crampton could be given his come-uppance into the bargain, then so much the better.

Talking of skins, I suddenly remembered Crampton's revolver. Where was it? Certainly not in his hand when I valiantly transported him to the sofa. I looked around the kitchen. No sign of the offending weapon on the table; nor on such available surfaces as the draining board, the washing machine, or the floor. I then did my favourite kitchen trick of tripping over the pedal bin, causing the lid to shoot open. Lo and behold. Crampton must have done the same thing ten minutes earlier. Down there among the tin cans and bottle corks, ensconced in a white polythene lining, was Crampton's revolver.

I tied up the polythene bag and dumped it outside the front door. No sign of Judith, who was presumably feeding herself somewhere. I then re-entered the house, intending immediately to go upstairs and reassure Terby that his life was out of immediate danger. My part in his rescue would at the very least afford Terby the obligation of keeping his mouth shut about my earlier contribution to the kidnapping. That was, if he found out it was me. At this stage all I intended to do was don my Edward Heath mask again, and write Terby some reassuring news on a piece of paper. But once again events proved to be running ahead of me. Even as these thoughts were running through my mind, from upstairs there came the unmistakeable shout of 'Tarquin! Tarquin!'

33

I had another quick look to make sure Crampton was out for the count, then dashed upstairs, no need of the mask, and confronted my old friend.

He was a pathetic sight – strapped to the bed, stripped of the professional armour which normally made him such an heroic figure in the paper-weight descriptions of financial journalists – my colleagues; myself. Where, I thought, are your assets now, Derek Terby? What help to *you* are your nominee holdings and your pyramidal balance sheets? What, for that matter, do you think your chances are *now* of realising that great ambition of becoming a real industrialist?

How often, in times past, I would have given anything for the opportunity to corner Terby in this way and say such things aloud. But I couldn't bring myself to do it, even as a sick game before revealing that I was on his side after all. There was no hostility on that oh so familiar fourth-form face; no anger: just fear and pained incredulity.

'*You*, Tarquin?' (Et tu Brute).

'Me, Terby,' I replied, keeping very much to myself the fact that the 'you' had the piercing force of a javelin. It wasn't for me to admit the implication that there was betrayal in the air.

'How did you know it was me?' I asked.

'When . . . the other fellow . . . shouted.'

'Oh.' Crampton's mannerism of calling people by their name in nearly every sentence. He'd managed to avoid referring to me as Tarquin during most of the escapade, but not when he reached breaking point.

Terby was understandably showing signs of exhaustion. He wasn't in any state to question me about the kidnapping, or the share price. All he wanted was his life.

'I can save you Terby, and maybe at some future date I'll explain my role in all this, which is not quite what you may think. But . . .' He nodded. No doubt he could see the 'but' coming a mile away, plus what followed. '. . . but until that future date you are in no way to communicate to *anyone* the fact that you know I'm involved.'

Terby nodded – insofar as anyone can when tied down to a bed like that.

'You do understand, don't you Derek?'

'Yes.'

'It may take twenty-four hours.'

'I . . . under . . . stand.'

I made sure Terby's door was closed this time, then went downstairs and re-entered the sitting room. Crampton was still flat out, snoring away, looking set for another eight hours. I woke him up gently, in accordance with the liberal methods prescribed for criminals nowadays. After a few 'whereami's' and 'wassamarrer's?' he focused on me.

'Tarquin. What happened?'

'There was a noise. In the garden. Remember? You sent me to investigate. It was just a cat. When I came back you were paralytic, collapsed in a heap. I brought you in here to make you comfortable.'

'Christ. Where . . . where's my gun?' Crampton had sobered up fast.

This was the opportunity for my master stroke. 'Terby's got it,' I lied.

'What? Have you gone stark raving mad?'

'No, I haven't. But you nearly did, Crampton. If you panic like that again, we'll both be finished. The whole basis of our operation is that – as you said in your house the first time – we only arouse the *suspicion* that Terby's dead.'

'That's all very well. But how the hell did Terby get hold of

161

my gun. Where is he?'

'The answer in both cases is simple. He's still upstairs, and I gave it to him. He's still bound up, but I loosened his right hand, so that if you so much as enter his room he'll shoot you. After what you threatened earlier he'll regard it as self-defence.'

Crampton was speechless for a few minutes. Not only had I taken over the initiative, but I had done so, as far as he was concerned, by assuming the officer-like qualities of which he thought he had the monopoly in our partnership.

I continued: 'I did this to help you. He can't escape, and you won't ruin everything by shooting him.'

'Rubbish. I merely have to get hold of another gun.'

'He's got orders from me to shoot first.'

Crampton looked more hopping mad than ever. Then he came back to the main point.

'What about the share price?'

'I will see that that comes tumbling down in the next twenty-four hours.'

'How?'

'With the aid of the media I work for, of course.'

Crampton paced up and down the room, very sour indeed. Finally he said: 'I'll give you until midday tomorrow to come up with some reassuring news. Otherwise we shall have to try something drastic. We've only got three days.'

'Goodnight Crampton and relax. I'll ring you at midday.'

34

I have a low boredom threshold. Long books – be they John Le Carré or Proust – just don't get finished in my household. There are at least thirty volumes hanging around my study to which I personally shall never return.

I have tried therefore in this account to apply my own criteria to the reader: I don't want to lose him or her before Tattenham Corner. If I have gone on a bit about events in the Surrenden Road house, forgive me. It just seemed to be one of the more interesting evenings in my life. But relax: we're now well into the home straight, and there's one minor bit of sex thrown in for the ailing prurient.

It occurred to me, as I shot through the door of the Folkestone house, that Terby hadn't even attempted to offer me money in return for his promised deliverance. A true sense of priorities I thought. My meditation on this subject nearly made me omit a vital part of the operation – picking up the polythene rubbish bag containing the revolver from just outside the front door.

'You must have a tale to tell,' said Judith as I hopped into the Mini.

'What can I expect in return?' I asked lasciviously.

'That depends on the tale,' she said, adjusting her jumper in the way women do, a way of drawing attention to the bosoms we never take our eyes off anyway.

She ignored my first grope. 'What have you got in that disgusting bag Tarquin?'

'A fire-arm. This could be rape.'

'Oh shut up you idiot. Whatever it is, it stinks. Well we'd

better dump it fast.'

I chose a terrace in the main road where the dustbins had been put out overnight. The bag was duly dumped and we headed out of town.

It was a very warm night – balmy in fact. I said: 'I want you.'

'I can't face going all the way back to London. Let's stop at a motel.'

Let's face it – motels, hotels: they always add an air of excitement to sex. The place we stopped at just about qualified for the title 'motel', having, so far as I could detect, room for three cars in the forecourt. The night porter added the sense of occasion by giving us that once over which suggests they're convinced it's your first time with this particular partner. Why, young people have to turn fifty before they can convince the average motel they're married, by which time the suspicion is they're married to someone else.

Since that weekend trip to Wales, when we had laid the ghost of Glyndebourne, it had been a case of getting straight down to it. Tonight I was continuing to live in the world of deals, however.

Judith stripped to her underwear – no further. Don't get me wrong – we displayed love, affection etc and fondled each other. At least I was under the impression we did. We lay down on the bed, literally resting, and I gave her an account of the evening's events.

'So you've got them there as your house guests Tarquin – each afraid of the other, and both depending on you?'

'Yes,' I said, not without a trace of smugness I fear.

I took the opportunity to remove her bra. These things always have to be done casually, I thought to myself.

'So how do you see it ending?'

'Down here, I hope. Oh, I see. Well . . .'

She looked pensive. The last surreptitious removal operation was nicely under way when she suddenly got up, pulled up her knickers again, and started walking around the room. Oh well, I thought. Wales was delirious. So was our little midday episode in Godfrey Street the day before. This was worth waiting for.

'Tarquin, there's something I ought to tell you.'

'Eh, what?' This ominous, but if there were any pregnancies in the offing they couldn't possibly have anything to do with me at this stage.

'Tarquin, I'm going to America.'

'What? How do you mean? When? How long for?'

'I telephoned Daddy this evening. He's been offered a chauffeuring job by an Anglophile multi-millionaire. He's taking it, and we're all going to California for two years.'

She paused for breath. So did I. The Southfields family had always been so close that the idea of Mummy and Daddy wanting to take their twenty-two-year-old daughter with them didn't strike me as at all surprising. I had always admired Mr Southfields' unconventionality. But, given the general direction in which my relationship with Judith had been drifting, I thought her decision somewhat cavalier to say the least.

I was aware of the classic ploy of forcing a marriage decision by presenting the dramatic alternative of a three-thousand-mile separation, but although we had known each other a long time, we really hadn't reached crunch time in our resumed relationship. Indeed I found myself all too readily rationalising her decision for her.

'Well naturally I'm sorry. But we'll keep in touch. Two years is a short time in sexual politics. I hope you have a marvellous time.

She stopped strolling up and down the room. She came over to the bed, took off her knickers with great deliberation, and said: 'All right, get on with it. But you might have shown *some* regret.'

35

Call it a sign of maturity, immaturity or just human nature, I found myself already thinking of the potentialities of that young divorced mother in the basement of Crampton's house as I drove Judith up to London from the motel the following morning. We said a reasonably fond goodbye in a traffic jam as she got out to catch a tube train, and I headed straight for the underground car park at London Wall. It was hardly worth driving up to the Canonbury Square flat since it was nearly Tring's conference time already. I might just as well grab some breakfast in one of those snackbars around Moorgate.

I bought the papers and glanced through them over breakfast. So much had happened in the last twenty-four hours that it was difficult to believe the *Jet*'s piece on industrial production was actually mine and written the evening before. That Wednesday morning's papers were full of other news – Vietnam, the east-west nuclear balance, a trade-union conference and yet another report on comprehensive schools. It wasn't the sort of day when Fleet Street was interested in blowing up City stories, and on the whole the Terby disappearance was being given the silly season treatment.

I took stock of the situation. The silly season treatment couldn't go on much longer. Meanwhile I was faced with the task of producing something to keep Crampton happy with my promised midday phone call. I was now committed to saving Terby – which, when the market realised he was all right would lead to a revival in the share price. But Crampton must get his comeuppance, which would also follow if Terby was seen to be okay, and Terby Holdings revived before Crampton had a chance to buy them at the low price he was after.

As for the 'incentive' Crampton had offered me, I had better remember to buy the equivalent of the line of shares sold in my name at £2.40 while they were still below this figure. Which left the number one question: just how, in the sober light of morning was I going to deal with Crampton? How, for example if I tipped off the police and got the Surrenden Road house raided, was I going to avoid being destroyed by Crampton, who, with the departure of the Southfields, would be the only man in England who knew about my coup? In the past twenty-four hours I'd been behaving like your typical British prime minister, quite quick on immediate tactics, but not knowing where they took you, and certainly devoid of strategy.

By the time I got into the *Jet* office, it was already conference time. Tring was saying to Spick: 'That piece about Terby Holdings got buried I'm afraid this morning. But we must really go to town on it tonight. What price are the shares now?'

'Still the overnight price of £2.25.'

'What do you reckon they'd be worth if Terby was found dead?'

'Well they were £2 for weeks before the bid was announced, and £1.95 just beforehand.'

Tring answered his own question. 'Without that spiv Terby I should think his little paper empire is worth no more than £1 a share if that. As for the Amalgamated bid, that of course would go by the board. We must write this tonight.'

Spick nodded obediently.

Tring turned to me. 'Tarquin, *you've* known Terby for years. Any idea where he might be skulking, or who would want to remove him from the scene?'

'None whatever, Augustus.'

Conference broke up at 11.20, leaving me with one or two things on my mind. Unfortunately it was a talkative morning – one could divide days on the *Jet* into those when people came out of conference and spent the rest of the time either out of the office or on the telephone, and those when they just nattered among themselves.

I checked the tapes – no more news of Terby – and rang Harry White – no more news either. The noise in the office was intolerable.

I rang Hopkirk and Grote, John Crampton's stockbroking firm. 'What is the price of Terby Holdings now?'

'£2.20 sir.'

'Now. That's quick. Buy fifty thousand in the name of T. A. R. Quin.' (Icy pause.) 'I'm a client of John Crampton, through whom I sold fifty thousand last week.'

'Hold on a minute sir. We'll check our records.' (An eternity of three minutes followed.) 'Are you there sir? Yes, that's right sir. Fifty thousand sold in your name at £2.40, and bought in your name at £2.20 today.'

'Right, please send contract note and all further details to me at 133a Godfrey Street, SW3.'

A little detail perhaps, but it was worth £10,000 to me on top of the £100,000 or so I had already made through my own coup. And it was £10,000 made available by Crampton – the incentive he had given me to play along with his kidnapping scheme.

Crampton had conducted his short selling of Terby Holdings when the price was in the £2 region. He couldn't buy the shares yet. Or rather, he could, but he wouldn't cover his losses.

Crampton, Crampton. It was now 11.50 a.m. and I'd promised to ring him with reassuring news at midday. Just then my telephone rang. It was Lord Brachan – himself, no secretary as intermediary.

'Tarquin, I wonder whether you could come round and see me at three p.m. It is a matter of some urgency.'

Memories of that extraordinary interview with Brachan as recently as yesterday. Goodness me, little Tarquin *was* in demand by the City Establishment. He might not have become a doctor, as his primary school teacher had prophesied, but he was seeing plenty of Lord Brachan.

'Of course, Lord Brachan.'

I rang Crampton. 'The shares are down another 5p. Have patience. By the end of this afternoon we'll have them below £2. Sorry, I must rush.'

Quite how I *was* going to have good news for Crampton at the end of the afternoon was another matter. I looked at my desk diary: due for lunch with a firm of stockbrokers at 1 p.m. I whizzed out of the office and grabbed a cab to 133a Godfrey Street, via the Embankment. All the 'sell' notes from my personal coup had now arrived intact. The profit would be about £110,000, plus the £10,000 or so I had just made in the 'bear' operation initiated on my behalf by Crampton, and completed that morning. Roughly £120,000, minus the capital gains tax I had no intention of paying. All set for a comfortable life in the Dordogne where, according to the property column in the previous Saturday's *Financial Times*, I'd be able to pick up a decent place for £5,000 or so. Shove it in a French bank and live on the proceeds. Charity begins abroad.

While waiting for a taxi in the King's Road I bought an irresistible airline-style bag from a spiv: inscribed 'Karate Club of Europe', it seemed a useful deterrent to muggers now that I was a man of means.

The brokers' lunch was notable for two developments: first a variety of rumours about Terby and Terby Holdings which were so contradictory that the share price remained solidly at the £2.20 it had edged down to earlier in the morning, not nearly good enough from Crampton's point of view, but increasingly worrying for Blizzards, whose reputation was at stake in this deal. Secondly, the news from the tapes – brought in during the first course, and causing a scramble for telephones on the part of the assembled brethren – that the pound was falling and that 'Whitehall sources' were not dismissing out of hand a sudden crop of rumours about a mini-budget. That was a bit of a professional shock for me. It was my job in the *Jet* office above all else to keep an eye on the economy; but I had been so preoccupied with my own personal economy in the past few days that I was a bit out of touch with my deep-throated contacts in Whitehall. But what the hell would that matter in the Dordogne?

36

It was 3.10 p.m. I was standing in the ante-room to Lord Brachan's office having arrived on the dot of 2.59 in response to Lord Brachan's urgent pre-lunch summons. 'I'm sorry about this Mr Quin,' said a receptionist who had obviously been schooled not to be too solicitous, but who displayed consciousness of the training in her very manner.

Brachan came in looking somewhat flustered. When he saw me I detected a feeling of embarrassment that he had been caught in a demeanour I did not associate him with. We – certainly he – may meet hundreds of people over the years, but we remember remarkably well the particular relationship we have with each one.

He was saying – not to me but to his secretary: 'I was delayed at the bank. Can you put back my appointments by a quarter of an hour?'

Then to me: 'Tarquin, how nice of you to spare the time to visit us. Do please come in.'

No sooner had he ushered me in and sat down himself, than the familiar flunkey came in with a piece of tape. This was becoming more and more intriguing. Your second rater will welcome any sort of interruption when he has a visitor, in a pathetic attempt to convince the audience of his importance. The really powerful man however, has the muscle to scare all interruptions away – unless, that is, there is a real crisis.

Brachan looked at the tape, and passed it across to me.

'You see what's happening to sterling Tarquin? It's very disturbing indeed. I wonder what's caused it.'

'A delayed reaction to the trade figures, maybe?' I ventured, remembering how Tring had insisted on being cheerful about some appalling figures a few days earlier – the figures which had perhaps precipitated the speculation about a mini-Budget.

'H'm,' said His Lordship enlighteningly. There was a long silence, during which Brachan affected to take a great interest in his air-conditioning apparatus.

Then he carried on, as if to himself: 'A scandal like this would do sterling no good at all. No good at all.'

Scandal? Sterling? I must confess that my initial fascination with this pillar of the merchant banking world was fading somewhat. So far from being spellbound by Brachan's words, his manner, his movements, my mind was wandering to the subject of Crampton, and just how I was going to sort out my little problem in Folkestone. I had done a deal with Terby, but was no nearer a resolution of Crampton's part in the affair. Then it hit me. I had taken Brachan to refer to being delayed at 'the bank'. But to a man in Brachan's position there were only two institutions that he would refer to as 'the bank' in that context. If he had just been at, say Rothschilds, or Barclays, he would have referred to them by name. There was only one 'bank' he would refer to like that – one could imagine him, on being late at a reception, saying, 'Sorry, I was delayed at the bank', meaning *his* bank, Blizzards.

Or ... It wasn't a 'bank' but 'Bank'. The Bank of England. Well, there were all sorts of reasons why Brachan could have been at the Bank; but it was at least possible that they were connected with the sterling crisis; or with the Terby/Amalgamated deal arranged by Blizzards, which was not looking too good at the moment; which he had talked about in vague but menacing connections the night before; which was what, in my heart of hearts, I was expecting him to talk about this afternoon:

'Tarquin, I like you.'

(Oh good)

'You remember what we were discussing last night?'

(*We*?) I nodded

'Tarquin, there are some very disturbing things happening at the moment.'

(You mean the pound's going down again? 'Tell me something new,' was what I would have said to my less illustrious friends.)

'Er, yes.'

'It is true that distasteful things happen in the City from time to time.'

'Yes.'

'And ideally the culprits ought to be punished.'

I hesitated to say 'yes' at this point, not being one hundred per cent certain of standing on holy ground.

'Any scandal involving the City could be very unfortunate for sterling at the present time.'

'Yes.'

'Confidence is a tender plant. Sometimes a run on the pound can get out of hand because it is associated – quite irrationally, perhaps – with other, concurrent problems.'

'Yes.'

'So far the market, in its usual sleepy way, does not seem entirely cognisant of the ...' – he hesitated – 'of the *problems* which appear to have arisen.'

'No.'

'But any minute ...'

There was a very long pause this time. I didn't know *how* the old devil knew, or what he knew. But the combination of the elliptical conversation the previous evening and this one was too much.

'Can I have time to think?'

He looked at his watch. 'About two minutes.'

It was now 3.30 p.m. Crampton would have been on the line frequently to his firm. The shares were still too high for him to cover his huge losses, let alone make any profit out of the kidnapping. My gut feeling was that the relatively small further fall in the share price would only revive Crampton's panicky condition: Terby was now in considerable danger.

I sensed that right there, on the other side of Lord Brachan's antique desk, lay a solution.

'My problem is that, if I help you, I shall need assistance myself.'

Brachan didn't exactly say 'tut tut', but he shook his shoulders in a manner which suggested the mere thought that I would not receive help in return a sign of bad breeding. He then waved his hand, and said in the softest tone of voice I had yet heard from him: 'My dear boy . . .'

I gave Brachan the exact address of the house in Folkestone. I explained that Terby had one captor, who was becoming increasingly edgy. I didn't think he was armed, but I couldn't be sure.

Brachan said: 'Good day to you Tarquin. You are very kind.' The flunkey showed me out.

37

Yes, there is a last chapter. There may even be another one. Believer in brevity that I am, I wasn't going to leave you in the dark like all those playwrights who finish their story in the middle of the last act. You know the sort: the audience is waiting for the final scene when suddenly the curtain rises and the actors (often as embarrassed as the audience) have to come forward to signal it's applause time. Off go your little after-theatre restaurant parties, each member sure of only one thing – that his IQ will be considered to have slipped if he doesn't attempt to explain the inexplicable.

I left Lord Brachan's magnificent office that Wednesday afternoon knowing that things were now entirely in his hands. In fact that was about all I did know. No sooner had I got out into the street than I realised that not for the first time in my life, it had been one of those conversations where I had left several things too vague – in the way one does when talking to such masters of obfuscation. In particular, I hadn't emphasised enough that it really could be a matter of hours before Crampton went over the top. And that was always assuming that my bluff had been successful and that Crampton had carried on believing my tale that Terby, as opposed to the local dustman, now possessed the gun.

When I got back to the *Jet* office I dithered between ringing Brachan to ram the point home, and telephoning Crampton with another delaying tactic. But I could hardly get away with a brief call like the one at midday. By now Crampton would want results – or an explanation for their absence.

I decided to ring Blizzards. But even as I reached for the telephone, I felt the clammy hand of Fate intervening in the shape of Augustus Tring, my boss.

'Why didn't we have the scoop on the mini-Budget Tarquin?' the little man said from behind my left shoulder.

'Well it's not absolutely certain that it's expected even now.'

'You must be the only person in ze world who isn't absolutely expecting it,' came the reply, a combination of screaming tones and the brief lapse into German pronunciation assuring me that this was not one to be wriggled out of easily. 'Come into my office.'

'I was just going to . . .'

'Just going to nothing. Come on.'

The next twenty minutes consisted of a harangue from Tring on what did I think he hired me for if not for being first with the economic news. I did not want to have to explain my preoccupation with my own personal economic news, so we had one of those routine slanging matches which preserve the dignity of human relationships.

By the time I was dismissed from Tring's presence it was 4.15 p.m. The main source of concern now was Crampton. But I had first to make a few calls to my contacts – official and unofficial.

I wanted to know the real extent of the pressure on sterling, and how accurate these reports on the tape were about an impending package of measures to protect the pound. It did not take long to discover that the pressure was there, and the reserve cupboard, if not exactly bare, was in need of replenishment. My best contacts, bless them, gave me a fairly full run-down of tax increases and public spending cuts under consideration – in the usual semi-code we had become accustomed to using over the telephone. Nearly all of them, however, dropped the hint that they thought the government could ride the situation out, and Ministers were very reluctant at this stage to go ahead with actually introducing the measures.

These calls done, I was now fully briefed for Tring's

5.30 p.m. conference. But my professional recovery programme had taken place at the expense of item number one. By now it was nearly five o'clock. Time I telephoned Blizzards.

'Lord Brachan's secretary.'

'Oh, it's T. A. R. Quin of . . .'

'Yes, Mr Quin, he's expecting you. I'll put you through.'

(Pause. Noises off. Sound of Brachan saying to someone else, 'You're so kind.')

'Tarquin. How kind of you to telephone. What can I do for you?'

'It's about the matter we were discussing earlier.'

'Which matter is that?'

(Oh, really, Lord Brachan . . .) 'Terby and the house in Folkestone. I wasn't sure whether I had stressed the urgency enough.'

'My dear Tarquin. Your meaning was very evident to me. I can assure you that everything is under control. I shall be in touch with you shortly.' (Pause. Sound of Brachan saying, 'Oh thank you. Yes, they seem to have got it right', then . . .) 'Do take a look at the Reuter tape timed 4.47 p.m. Tarquin. Good day to you.'

I didn't need to. As I came off the telephone I heard Jack Spick complaining: 'Bloody hell. I knew it all along. Here's Tring wasting my time with this rubbish about what Terby's shares would be worth without Terby, and there's no mystery at all. I could have been doing that press release for the *Workers' News*. Terby's just been quoted at London Airport saying he doesn't know why the shares have fallen, and early soundings indicate overwhelming support for the deal from the key institutional shareholders.'

38

I lived in limbo for the next fortnight. No Judith. No Mrs Cordoba. Enough time to keep myself and *Jet* readers informed on the minutiae of the government's internal battle over new measures – the probability of which seemed to recede daily as sterling staged a recovery in the light of odd bits of good economic news. But all the time my thoughts were, as they say, elsewhere.

There was plenty of visible news on the Terby front: the shares went back to £2.35 – not the bid price of £2.45 because the market in general did not recover fully from the sterling scare. Lots of smiling pictures of Terby. A well-orchestrated publicity machine keeping the papers happy daily with the news of how more and more insurance companies and pension funds were clambering on to the Terby bandwagon.

But the orchestra's conductor himself was missing: Terby may have been readily available to the world, but Lord Brachan's way of getting in touch with me 'shortly' was to take a holiday in the Seychelles, leaving his deputy to get on with the perform-ance. As for me, I may have been scared stiff that the long arm of the law was about to land on my shoulder, but my 'understand-ing' had not been with Brachan's deputy, and my questions just had to wait. Lacking any reassurance from Brachan, I was also apprehensive about the long arms of both Terby and Crampton. But there was no word from them; and you can guess who wasn't going to make overtures about the resumption of diplomatic relations.

My feeling of being in limbo was such that there was an air of unreality about what should have been the high spot of the fortnight – not to say my entire adult life. That was when I got my socialist hands on the various cheques totalling nearly £120,000 which comprised the proceeds of my coup plus the extra from the 'incentive' Crampton had given me. Don't get me wrong: I didn't exactly tear them up after all that devoted effort. It was just that without talking to Brachan I could never know how safe I was.

But with a great sense of timing, Lord Brachan made his promised telephone call to me later on the same day as the brokers' cheques arrived. It was something of a privileged call: an invitation to breakfast at 8.30 a.m. the following morning.

Brachan lived, I now discovered, in one of those Kensington houses which put even Brompton Square into the shade. All the best Georgian houses are so unobtrusive in their elegance that the uninitiated hardly notice what they're missing. On this occasion, however, I was ushered through the house so fast that there was hardly time to bump into the furniture. The Portuguese maid outdid her boss in anxiety: I spent a good ten minutes admiring His Lordship's roses and vines before Brachan emerged for breakfast on the patio.

He was wearing a silk dressing gown and a pair of those Indian-style sandals which are all the rage among the Afghan-shirt set. No doubt they had been picked up in the Seychelles for a song. His lean, angular face – still very handsome for a man of sixty or so – was heavily sun-tanned. I didn't know where Lady Brachan fitted into the scheme of things, but I think it was somewhere in Wiltshire. Brachan was looking almost rakish, and I guessed that somewhere upstairs there lay his Seychelles companion.

He found me admiring his vines. 'They're not bad, Tarquin, are they? One is meant to have to choose between the length of the vine and the quality of the fruit, but these days in London the weather seems to provide both. Sit down, dear boy, and Maria will bring us some coffee.'

Maria brought us coffee all right. She also brought us orange juice, grapefruit, bacon and eggs and – well, yes, she did: a bottle of champagne.

'Forgive this extravagance Tarquin, but I feel we have something to celebrate.'

It was all very British. During my journalistic career I had several times breakfasted at Claridge's with American bankers whose names are household words; but I didn't enjoy such occasions a bit, because of the intensity with which they and their aides insist on getting down to business before you've had time to breathe. Don't they realise that in a declining nation we like to take our time about these things? Here I was, agog to hear Lord Brachan's news, but civilisation was the order of the day, and we got the main subject via a digression on inflation in Diocletian's time, an analysis of Olivier's performance in *Long Day's Journey*, and Lord Brachan's views on Tolstoy, with whom he'd been dabbling in the Seychelles when not dabbling with you can guess what.

'Now, Tarquin.'

(Now, Lord Brachan.)

'Tarquin, have you ever thought of a job at Blizzards?'

(Eh? What?)

'Er, how do you mean?'

'What I say. A job at Blizzards.'

'Well, I mean, I, er . . . What makes you . . . ? I'm just a . . .' (I'd heard of people being recruited for MI5 like this, but this was ridiculous.)

Brachan sighed. 'We're all in the information business Tarquin. That's why I myself was asked to join Blizzards. That's why I want you to join us. Think about it, anyway.'

Brachan dropped the subject and raised his glass.

'Let us, at all events, drink to the success of our recent dealings.'

There was a long silence. I was by now bursting to hear him cough up with his side of the Terby information business. But it was one of those occasions when the best questioning technique is acquiescence in the long silence.

After a few minutes he got up and began to show an intense

interest in the nearest rose bush – an Albertine, I think. Then he replied to my unspoken questions. Even *he* could not resist talking to *someone*.

'The Kent police had no difficulty with Crampton. Five of them entered the house simultaneously through doors and windows, within half an hour of your visit to my office. That was a most helpful visit Tarquin.'

'You seemed to know quite a lot already, if I may say so. How?'

'I suppose this is why they pay me Tarquin. I'm hardly a young man, I don't think I did too badly in the circumstances. We had a lot of discussions at Blizzards, and were constantly in touch with the police about Terby's disappearance. But nobody else seemed to concur with my interpretation of events.'

'And you? How did you know?' I was aware that this was pushing it a bit. (The beauty of the British Establishment is that it moves in mysterious ways, and seldom explains itself.)

'I *didn't* know, Tarquin. It just seemed to me that anybody with any sense would not have kidnapped Mr Terby for ransom money, but for the effect such an event might have on the share prices. I may say that I was on my own in holding this view. None of the highly paid young men at Blizzards agreed with me. So much for university education and business schools.'

'Didn't you have *any* evidence for this?'

'None whatsoever. But my theory did point to Mr Crampton, whose bearish views on Terby Holdings are well known – views which have indeed, been propounded all too often by that gentleman within the walls of my own bank.'

I wondered whether he had taken me for a ride with all those heavy hints about the effect on sterling if the Terby kidnapping developed into a major scandal. He could see the way my mind was working.

'I can assure you, Tarquin, that I did not deceive you about the view – it was, indeed, shared at both ends of town – that if the affair had been allowed to continue, the effect on the market could have been very bad for sterling . . .'

'Was it shared by you?'

He smiled wickedly, 'From my standpoint, the aspect which mattered most was the effect on Blizzards . . .'

All right. The old fox. But so what . . . provided he had done his stuff for me. But how had he known the connection between Crampton and me?

'I'm pleased you acted on my earlier hints to you about Terby and Amalgamated, Tarquin. The press can be very useful sometimes in bringing things out into the open. When there are difficulties behind a deal, there is nothing quite like the appearance of a fait accompli.'

By now I felt like a whole row of pawns in the Brachan chess game. But I still couldn't fathom how he knew about the connection between Crampton and me.

'I didn't Tarquin. I guessed that, with your advance information, you might have tried to make a little money on the side out of the Terby deal. And I took it that you would have a guilty conscience. But while I suspected Crampton had kidnapped Terby, I had no idea where he was, or of the connection between you two.'

'Really?'

'Really . . . But I assumed that as a diligent journalist you would not lose interest in the Terby story once it appeared that he had been kidnapped.'

I was sure now that I had credited Lord Brachan and his Establishment friends with rather more knowledge than they had actually had. But presumably, even if the rescued Terby had kept quiet about my part in the kidnapping, Crampton must have talked.

'You need have no worries about Crampton, Tarquin. He has lost a great deal of money out of all this.' (Good: come uppance is at hand . . .) 'But an understanding has been reached under which charges will not be preferred against him, provided you yourself come to no harm. It would nevertheless be inadvisable, I should have thought, for you to go out of your way to meet him. The provocation might be too much.'

Understanding? The government, the City and the police

covering up another scandal ... The fact that the cover up helped *me* meant that I was hardly in a position to complain. But Brachan offered no further elaboration. When I pressed him he merely said: 'Some things, Tarquin, are best left unsaid. Preferring charges against a leading stockbroker for kidnapping one of our most distinguished business men' – I like to think Brachan had his tongue in his cheek at this point – 'Would have done no good for the City or the pound, at a time when criticism from the Left about the City appears to be in the ascendancy.'

So. The system I used to hate had come up trumps. I looked at Brachan, his garden and the remains of that delicious breakfast. I finished my champagne. I did not know whether to thank Brachan for his part in a deal which I knew had been advantageous to him anyway, or leave that unsaid.

'Another half bottle?' he said.

'Why not?'

'Why not indeed.'

'Your friend Mr Terby had a very nasty shock you know Tarquin. You really mustn't do anything like that to him again.'

(No, Lord Brachan.)

'There remains one thing. Are you sure you don't want a job at Blizzards?'

'Certain. I'm going abroad for a while.'

'Well, let me know if you change your mind.'

Brachan showed me to the door. I fancied I caught sight of his Seychelles companion floating down the stairs as I was leaving. When his secretary rang the *Jet* office later that day to ask if I knew of any other young men with journalistic experience who fancied a merchant banking job I actually thought of Jack Spick, believing that in any holocaust to come, Blizzards might well like to hedge its bets with a few Trots.

Jack's doing very nicely thank you – for Blizzards and himself. The Terby/Amalgamated went through, to the financial delight of Mrs Cordoba, whose estranged husband George went on the combined board. The products of Terby/Amalgamated are household words. The grovelling letter Terby wrote to thank me for his salvation – inspired by Lord Brachan? – is one of my most treasured documents.

Whether I emerge from this honest account as a likeable character or a bastard I leave the reader to judge. My final confession is : NO, I did not give any of my ill-gotten gains to charity; nor did I embark on the successful liberal political career of philanthropists who have made their dirty pile first. On the other hand, having made one system work for me, I was faced with the way the system itself had to contend with something else.

After a brief affair with the girl in Crampton's basement, I departed for the Dordogne with the odd £20,000 or so, leaving the balance of £100,000 in what I fondly thought to be the safe hands of Blizzards' investment department. Unfortunately I had chosen one of the worst moments in history to become a capitalist. Inflation halved the value of my ill-gotten gains within five years, then carried on.

I have enjoyed my French leave, but at this rate I shall soon be seeking gainful employment again – possibly at Blizzards where, now that Lord Brachan has retired on a pension which has also been hit by inflation, Jack Spick is my main link. Mrs Cordoba has re-established contact, and comes out to stay with me occasionally. It was she, it turns out, who was Lord Brachan's companion in the Seychelles. I still like to call her Mrs Cordoba and Starling; but technically she is now Lady Brachan.

Keegan, William
A real killing.